THANH DINH

Love, Anyways

Because the Apple Trees Blossom

First edition

ISBN: 978-1-0694998-7-5

Editing by Cynthia Constantino
Cover art by Tiago Araujo

This book was professionally typeset on Reedsy.
Find out more at reedsy.com

For Mr. Thanh Loc, my inspiration, and the flame within him that keeps on burning, despite the torrential falls from all sides.

Contents

Acknowledgments

Hi — it's been a long time. This is Thanh Dinh from Writerly Books.

This short story collection has come a very long way. Some stories were rejected. Some were accepted, only to be buried under a thick layer of dust. Let's just say the whole book is me reminiscing about a time when I wrote like a pretentious Virginia Woolf, thinking I, too, could win a Nobel. Vanity is nothing; lacking vanity is also nothing.

To make these stories shine as beautifully as they do now, I owe my sincerest gratitude to my editor, **Cynthia Constantino**. She elevated my creative process with insights I could never have seen on my own and helped refine the selection with precision and care. Without her, there would be no *Love, Anyways*—only more paper wasted on the empty vanity of a writer. Cynthia, if you're reading this, know that I adore the work you've done on this project. I hope you'll be there for the next book, the next of the next, and evermore.

Another person I want to recognize is my cover designer, **Tiago Araujo**. His work is extraordinary—he's a fiery, kind soul who understands every task with ease and lets his creativity blend seamlessly with the writer's vision. If you love the cover, please give him some love too.

And of course, my family—my mother, father, and sister—who have been with me longer than anyone, and who have suffered through the hardest moments when I was at my lowest. My friends, **Tam Nguyen** and **Hoang-Anh Nguyen**, who may joke about my career but are always the first to protect me whenever the world turns cruel.

I love you. I love all of you, truly. Thank you for tolerating my existence up to this moment—and even after it.

Burnin' Love

I sit down by the large, Baroque-style windows of the century-old tea shop. Outside, the evening is casting a gloomy shadow of a looming storm and soon, darkness will regain its throne. I pick up the menu. The corners are crumpled and the pages are growing yellow from the flow of time that has passed and the slow, cruel hand of time that will be passing by. I doubt that another thousand years will fly through the Baroque-style windows, and I will always be here. Solitude will always be here.

The tea selection is as broad and varied as always, but both the master and I know that only a few of them are available. I tap on the *genmaicha* item twice. The master nods knowingly then go back to cleaning the silver spoons and the fragile china pieces on the countertop. He knows who I am waiting for. I know what I am yearning for. Both have little to do with genmaicha, or the little teapot with the rising scent of burned rice grains. I breathe in, relish the feeling of living, of existing here, all alone, when everyone outside is just passing by. Their shadows catch on the stained-glass windows, the same faces, the same look in their eyes, as if they are manufactured in the same factory. Only one of them is different. And that one has yet to come here.

L., I wonder where you have been after your scandal with the city theater. They told me many things when I was still struggling to get a bit of money to send you. Pretty things. Nasty things. As if I will believe their little lies over your magnanimous presence in my memory.

Coughing, I pull the tattered, red wallet out of my dirty canvas bag. The vibrant red color has long since faded into a deep, muddied burgundy. The gilded clasp has lost its shine, and the gold button is already twice broken. But no matter.

Inside the wallet are the stubs of two tickets to a stage play. *A Beastly Contract,* it says. The date and time for the play are no longer there but they are carved deeply into my brain. In the empty tea shop, I drown in the mournful, raspy voice of Khanh Ly, relishing the things I lost. What I once treasured, as if it was my only reason for living: what I had once promised to protect, even if the cost for it was my existence. In the end, the words and vows become nothing more than dust covering L.'s ivory mantelpiece in the setting of a stage play.

But whenever I close my eyes, the lights were on, and there L. was, standing in the spotlight in a white suit as the auditorium darkened, his back turned to the audience. The theater was filled with a pregnant silence.

Holding my breath behind the wings to check the sound quality, I could hear the protagonist's voice ringing, "But I loved you." He lowered his head on the word "love," and I wondered how much solitude a shoulder could hold. Then L. stepped away from the stage. Unconsciously, as if on cue, I stood up from my control seat, my lips quivered, my hands reached out, my whole skeleton trembled. *Don't go,* I mouthed to the darkening stage. The curtain was drawn, and it was too late. The last standing ovation for a superb performance of a man in drag. Ten minutes into midnight, and the applause kept going until I was the only person living in the dying limelight. Turning the control board off, I immersed myself in the ocean of love between me and the star I could never reach.

But I can't live with closed eyes forever. The next moment I open them, the tea shop is there. An eternity has passed in ten minutes, but we are not born to live forever. What I have left to relish at the moment are a photo of him and me, and the ticket stubs from that day. How long has it been since the genesis happened and he breathed life into me? How much longer can I hold onto this agony, sitting here, closing my eyes, watching the back of his white suit fading into the darkening theater until life starts to flow again? And the audience will live, while in that little corner behind the curtain, I died a million times, wishing I could live in that tiny frame of five-minute epilogue until my soul burns in hell for the sins I have committed. Vanity is nothingness. Lack of vanity is also nothingness.

"Master, do you know if Mr. L will come today?" I ask, not expecting an answer.

"I don't know, ma'am. He never gives prior notice," the master replies, not caring if his words will cause hurt.

"How long have you known Mr. L, master?"

"Who has the time to count those things, ma'am?" The master laughs. "Ten? Twenty? Thirty years? All I know is on the day I opened this shop, he sat there, in the seat you are sitting in."

"He always loves watching the city and the neon lights. He was born for it," I say. A bitter taste rises in my throat and blooms on my tongue, but all I can feel is a sweetness so hot it smolders on my lips.

"You seem to know him well," the master says with thinly veiled curiosity. "How long have you known him then?"

"How long do you think?" I sip the burning tea, watching the people rushing by. The streetlights slowly light up and the traffic lights change constantly, but he is never there.

"You seem too young to know him for long. I would guess about ten years."

"Perhaps," I say absentmindedly and take out the photo of us. The borders are curved, and his smile is lost to time. "As you say, who has the time to count those things?"

The master stays silent. The only sound is the squeak of clean cloth on fine china and silverware. And I sit there, getting lost in the past that is too fresh to be buried, but too painful to dig up for a healing session on a sunny day. Is it my luck that the weather is gloomy today or is it the remnant of his last mercy on my beating heart?

This is Main Street, the upper part. Cross a few blocks and we will come to the intersection of a secret lane, leading to where the shabby theater once stood, the light shining every night. There used to be a cafe there, serving superb desserts and sweet treats but he never had the taste for those. I remember he once told me, "Don't get the cakes there. They're cold. Get the ones from the small bakery next door. I know you'll like them better."

"But how do you know?" I asked.

"I just have that intuition," he said, brushing through his eyebrows, preparing for another tragic act. His hair was slicked back, pomaded. His eyes sparkled with the glaring white ring lights. He drew on wrinkles and his pallor was paler than ever. And I thought, *But darling, you were never more beautiful.* The past was always a never-ending fairy tale, but I doubted then, as I doubt now, that I would be the one living to hear him tell the tales of his holy cathedral—the theater. The stage was on, and I was only a comical version of a person amidst the crowd of people passing the crossroad.

"I will get the cakes from that bakery from now on, then," I said, checking the monitor, the sound system, and the lighting. No one was allowed to outshine my angel of darkness as long as I worked there at the city theater.

"Darling, I will die before everything ends, won't I?" he asked jocosely and put down the eyebrow powder. His face was serene, his hands clasped on the makeup table, and his eyes looked straight into the mirror, drowning in the sadness and solitude that only he knew. "They said I had the eyes of a heartbroken widow."

He often got into that mood. When I went on break with my tech team, they made jokes about his whimsical depressive talks. I laughed at some of them and carried the rest on my shoulders. Born from a traditional artistic family, he made his name after the wars by rebelling against the system. When the government saw how dangerous the situation would be to let his light shine too bright on the dimness of the stillborn citizenship, he was castaway: no one bothers to remember his family's sacrifice; neither does they care about his artistic ambition. He becomes an eyesore, forever being suppressed by the government he had trusted.

Did he ever feel lonely? I asked him once, twice, or many times. He shook his head, accepting the defeat, saying he couldn't go on fighting a rebellion where there would be no victor in the end. He was fine because he had acting. I wondered if he ever heard my heart shatter when he talked that way.

Did I want him to feel lonely? He asked me in turn. His eyes were like two mirrors reflecting my black soul.

"Yes," I replied, "because at least then you will need me." He waved my pessimism away, saying that there would come a day when I wouldn't need him or anyone to live happily.

Between us were thirty years of pain, suffering, and agony. He had been through enough to forgive life. I hadn't learned my lesson of letting go yet.

"Oh, but you won't, you won't." Trying to console him from the stark truth we both knew and couldn't change, I repeated these words like the naïve idiot that I always was in his presence. "And your eyes are beautiful. And you are beautiful. And we will live. And you will act; oh, how you will act, again and again and again." I broke down mid-sentence into tears. But he just smiled through and through. At that time, he was nearly sixty years old. The shadow of death was knocking on his door every night like a close friend. I was thirty. My life had just begun. But my love had grown large enough to shelter both of us. Or at least, that's what I believed.

"Master, do you suppose the city theater will survive another year?" I ask, not paying attention to the tea being served.

"I don't know, ma'am." The old master ponders. "I hear that they're building another one on top of the old place. Perhaps next year, the old city theater will be torn down."

"Does it have to be that way? Tearing down the past to build a new future, master, don't you think it is a form of erasure? Ten more years, and I will no longer remember the theater's shape." I reply absentmindedly, twisting my fingers, watching the backs of the passersby, thinking, reminiscing about his back in the white suit, fading, fading, fading into oblivion, darkness.

I think of the nightly acts. Cross the street, walk a few feet, turn into the back door, and there he is, putting on makeup for the nightly stage plays. I would tap him on the shoulders and he would drop everything he was doing to give me a warm hug. He would throw his arms around my waist, catching me in surprise. I would giggle, happily sticking my ears to his chest, listening to life's greatest music—the beating of his heart.

"Why are you here?"

"I thought of giving you a surprise."

"I am glad really—"

"I know."

"You'd have to wait but—"

"I know."

"How about the shop on N_____ street?"

"I'll wait there after the show."

"It will be late and—"

"I can wait. I can wait forever if you promise that you will always stay here."

"Of course. Where else do I belong?"

"And where else do you suppose I belong?"

These days, I often dream that he'll hug me again. In those dreams, I smell the faint scent of the thick face powder falling on his chest. The cologne he used smelled like crushed rose petals burned in sandalwood, and I still have an empty bottle of it sealed on my nightstand along with his wig, a hair pin, and the CD of his musical songs. For old time's sake.

Sometimes, the dreams are real enough that I can feel the beating of his heart through the thinly clothed skin; the warmth is spreading through our bones. He'd be heaving dramatically—as is his way of expressing his love—and breathing in the chemical scent of my shampooed hair. And only then, he'd let me go. I'd step out and leave the white peony bouquet on the boudoir, preparing for the beginning act, turning on the light, checking the sound system. He'd wave after me and

I'd smile at our last goodbye, because neither of us knew then when the next time would be. We lived on tiptoes, and we loved like burning matches: we always presumed that it was the end before it ever began. Where else do you suppose I belong? Where else am I hurt this bad? Where else do I still hold on, decade after decade, tide after tide, chasing, waiting, crying, reaching for something that was never promised to be mine in the first place? I have known you for my whole life and half of it has been spent chasing after the ghosts you made. And yet, how much solitude can a shoulder hold?

"Master, Mr. L will not come today, will he?" I ask, fully aware of the answer.

"Mr. L will come when he wants to come," the master replies, a tinge of pity and frustration in his voice.

After all, people come here often to search for that one person. That one star who outshines the rest. The name has become such a sensation, no one dares to whisper it in vain. And yet, how can I tell them it was I who first learned to love him the way the earth yearns for the moon?

"Say, master, do you think he will give up the stage?"

"After recent scandals about his defects and betrayals, I don't think he's ready to stand on the stage again soon."

"They are not the first scandals he had."

"And they won't be the last. But ma'am, the other day, when he came here, he said there's no saving it. The spilled water cannot be gathered up into the cup."

"That doesn't mean he will give up, does it?"

"Yes, ma'am. I suppose so. Everyone has their own idea of giving up, after all."

I sit there watching the clock's hands move slowly by. We hadn't seen each other in twenty-nine years exactly, to the date and the minute. Everyone trusts that a promise is made to be kept, no one knows when the betrayal takes shape behind the many twists and turns of life. Who amongst our old friends and colleagues guaranteed that he would come to this shop after all these years with a withered white peony bouquet to compensate for the time he made my skeleton tremble under my skin? The earth moved and without knowing it, I had let go of his hands for but a second, only to lose him forever. But it's him we are talking about. He would probably say, "It can't be helped because life is about losing everything." My eyes are wide open with tears. The ticket stubs are on the table. The red wallet is torn up at the corner. The photo grows blurry with time and eventually, he is no longer in the frame.

"Ma'am, the shop is closing."

"I know. But I'm still waiting."

"For what?"

"A promise."

Inside the vacant tea shop, the music slowly fades out into nothingness. The singer mourns, "Without you, I've been burnin' love." But perhaps he'd known. He'd always known far too well how to break a person's heart, only to build it up again, broken everywhere and broken in between, but it will be whole, the same shape and contour as the day he dropped it onto the cement floor and watched as I writhed in agony with my love for him. It's easy to break a person's heart. Like the day he walked through the door of the teashop when he finished his first show at the current theater. With a natural, innate gracehe strided to our usual seats. The warm voice retained the cheekiness of a young rebel he ordered the set of petit fours and another set of buttered scones because he knew I never liked sweets. He lifted his eyes, looking at me from underneath the quivering eyelashes, saying the line that would haunt me eternally: "I loved you."

"Why the past tense?" I said.

"Because the present hasn't happened yet."

"Do you still love me in the present then?"

"Darling, you're the one I could never stop searching for. What do you think?"

And my heart was breaking so his could live. My life was flowing from the stagnant stream of the barren river of the old years. Sweet as poison, bitter as blessings, L., you are my one and only burnin' love.

In the Box

They say that when you are in the box, the only way out is through. This school of thought stems from the fact that one has the certain knowledge that, without fail, outside the box, there is something else. Maybe people will reach hell. Most of them believe they will reach heaven. Those with little faith simply settle for the thought of an escape route. But then, one has to come to terms with this question before finally taking the jump, or the way through: If you don't know about the world outside the box, how can you be certain that you will be safe when you escape the prison you are living in?

Such is the current case of M., our protagonist.

M. wakes up in a state of confusion on a tiny bed that tightly squeezes his bony, human frame. He can barely stretch his legs because at the end of the bed is the wall; and if he stretches his arms to their full length, he reaches two other walls. He stands up. Underneath his feet is another wall—or a floor, in layman's terms—and just an inch above his hair is another wall, or the ceiling. "Damn," M. curses loudly, listening to his voice echoing through the four walls with a tinge of uncanny premonition, "Am I in some kind of weird dream? What happened to the house I was in? And what will happen to the job, the bills, the salary I'm going to get? Is it the end of the month yet? The wedding invitation of the boss's daughter! I need to get out of here."

With that train of racing thoughts, M. tries to find some opening, but there is none. It's a box made of cement, he mulls to himself, a box without a way out. An eternal prison. He thinks about the night before when he went to sleep, the preceding days, the world that keeps on moving outside without him, and without anyone noticing a missing person. The weird thing is, he cannot remember the world outside. What did he do before lying down to this intermittent death? He doesn't remember. Did he eat? What is eating? An act to satisfy hunger. Did he feel hunger raging within him before? He doesn't know. Crawling into a corner, scratching his head, M. finds that he is losing the thread connecting him to what he considers his life. Or what normal people and society define as a life. It is no use. He is stuck inside a limbo, and the more he stays, the more of himself he will lose. Looking at the dark, cement ceiling, he wonders from where this box is resurrected, and where it will go. He wonders if a box has enough conscience to understand the meaning of the word *destination*, and whether it has its own will to chart the course of its life. He chuckles, a spark of laughter in the dark, and no one will hear. *It is mad and ridiculous,* he thinks, *to imagine, even for a split second, that a box could think, could have its own will, could possess enough strength to alter the course of my life.* No one would believe that a mere box made of his delusional constraints in this nightmarish trap could maim and kill. He seems to float together with the box in the middle of nowhere. There are no beginnings; there are no ends. He strains his ears to listen, but no noise comes through. He rubs his face, burrowing it into his knees, wishing, knowing there's no chance of it coming true.

"Damn, what had I been thinking before this dream happened?"

To answer M.'s question, and to understand his case, we can go back to yesterday and peruse his daily activities to see the cause, the root of the problem, and to judge for ourselves whether this box is as much of a deserving punishment for him as he seems to think.

Though many people in his life have no knowledge of his ailment, since it is a stigma to talk about such peculiar cases, M. has long been a sufferer of schizophrenia and bipolar depression. He has been under the control of medication for more than twenty years. The only thing, or person, preventing him from being fully admitted to the inpatient department at the Central Mental Health Hospital is the old doctor who has been on his case since he was still a high school student. Many times, he has contemplated cutting the cord with life for good, and the image of the aging doctor bending over his diagnosis, glasses hanging on the bridge of his nose, meditating on the different kinds of medication, twitching his eyes, mulling over the best way to keep M. sane for a day longer, or a second longer, always holds him back. One time, when he overdosed, the old doctor almost decided to give up on him. "Listen," the old doctor said, "I won't be on this earth longer than ten more years. Fifteen, if we are being generous with my prediction about Alzheimer's disease, and you are not making things easy, Mr. M. I can't save someone who has already decided to surrender." And M. knew in that instant that the next time he was hospitalized, the doctor wouldn't be by his bedside. So he bit his tongue, put on the shackles, and together with the old doctor, slowly trudged through the mud.

But it all came crashing down yesterday, after the regular checkup. M. sat stiffly in the swivel chair, fiddling with the hem of his shirt, asking the doctor in an almost inaudible voice, as if each word was a bleeding stab in his flesh: "How long?"

"How long what, Mr. M.?" the doctor in the worn, white smock asked. His eyes twinkled with a tiny spark of intrigue.

"How long until it all ends?"

"I'm afraid I cannot answer that question, Mr. M." The old doctor lifted the glasses on his nose, trying to read the name of the latest medication change. "I see that you're not adjusting well to the new dosage. How about I adjust it a little?"

"I don't know. You're supposed to know my case well enough by now," M. said, his voice hollow.

"As I am supposed to know everyone else's case. You'd be amazed at how good one becomes at lying when one has done it for a long time."

"Doctor, sometimes, I have a suffocating feeling, like I'm living in a box."

"Well, if you think hard about it, we're all in a box of our own, in a way." The doctor turned around and looked with pity and benevolence at M. "You and I, we're all in a box. When you come to me, you're simply walking out of your box and walking into another's."

"People say there's an outside. The only way out is through."

"Mr. M., consider this." The doctor took off the glasses, folding his delicate hands on the table, brushing M.'s case aside with a sweeping movement. "To put it in your words, the world is made of boxes. Your suffering, your thinking, your ideologies, all the things that your mind constructs—they constrain you and make up your own box. I, too, have my own constraints and my own box. People say there is an outside because they never see the outside. They say to push through because they are yet to know what lies out there. Suppose the citizens at Troy knew what was hidden inside the wooden horse; would they still have accepted it and taken it in? It all comes down to how much pain you can tolerate. We all expect there to be an everlasting heaven and an everlasting hell. That's why people always try to push through. But that's not the point."

"Do you believe in there being an outside?"

"I haven't seen any 'outside' that's not nasty, and that is from me, who has stood on a high enough ladder to look down. Mr. M., to truly see the outside, you need the eyes of a god. A very callous, extremely cruel god in his own benevolent and selfless way. And think of it carefully, Mr. M, even God wants us to suffer." The doctor smiles, his eyes shining with a gentle gray color.

"Then I'd rather not leave my box."

"Who knows? Maybe when you're in the box long enough, you'll want to push through."

"And why is that?"

"Because it's in human nature to rebel. That's the point, Mr. M. That has always been the point."

And with that conversation in mind, perhaps we will read the story from the beginning once more with a new view on our protagonist's current state. But of course, to fit the narrative, he doesn't remember the conversation with the doctor. And to confuse him further, the author decides to not allow him the mercy of remembering his idea of not wanting to leave the box. So the only question in his head right now, the persistent desire, the relentless wish, the fervent prayer, keeps him pushing at the box's borders: Is there an outside?

He knocks on the wall. There's no response from the other side, and he has expected none from the start. *But what if the walls are soundproof?* he deludes himself. After hours of useless fighting, he walks back to where he began and lies on the bed, pondering an escape route, a feasible way to break the walls down. He reasons that no one has sufficient authority to force him to live inside this prison. That he has the right to—to do what? M. watches the blank walls around him and the void of human existence except for himself. He is comfortable here, M. thinks. He doesn't have any unfulfilled needs and thus, he doesn't feel the box lacking. But why, why is the void inside him growing larger and larger? He just needs to find the right words. He just needs to figure out the right cause for his action. "I have the right to—" he screams, but the box swallows his voice, and he catches onto it like a long-enduring, hungry child. The words stumble out of his mouth in a fit of passion. "I have the right to freedom." He pushes through the walls with his head and at the first impact, the walls crash. M. wakes up. Above him is the same ceiling. If he reaches out his arms, he can touch the walls. He looks to his side. The old doctor is standing over him, taking note of the statistics.

"Is this a dream?" M. asks, his breathing growing fainter with each beep from the heart monitor.

"Or is this a dream within a dream?" The doctor smiles with a grandiose benevolence Mr. M. has never seen in him before.

"I thought I chose freedom."

"But you pushed through to another prison. Let me tell you something—look not for freedom, for it's long gone."

"Then what should I have done?"

"Choose the prison. Your freedom lies in the right to choose the prison you live inside."

The old doctor walks away. M. looks at him. Everything inside him is white like the paint on the walls of the box in his dream. *Am I the one dreaming of the man in the box,* M. thinks, *or is he dreaming of me?*

The Death in the Garbage Truck

I t comes as no surprise to the poor, manual-labor town that N. dies in the garbage truck. In fact, everything is a foregone conclusion. A prophet once carved into the stone of the dark alleyway's molding brick walls: "The poor die first; the rich come later. Good people go under so evil can cross over." The blue-collar workers with black lungs and gritty fingers don't understand the gift of the prophet's meaning; eventually, his carving becomes a folklore that is passed down from generation to generation.

N.'s funeral happened on a dreary, rainy day. The words form on the tip of the withered, wrinkled old man's tongue and slither down the winding road of the shabby houses until a young child's eyes look up. The funeral hearse trudges by on its four muddy wheels and his mother sighs, "Well, there he goes." The journalist would pay to hear the tales these run-down walls and aluminum roofs have in their empty stomachs, but even if they could talk, the first thing on their mind and the last phrase on their lips would be *more money*. People in this little village can only fit so much time into their lives for eating, working, and lying awake at night, counting the mornings until the promised apocalypse.

According to the newspaper, half of N.'s corpse was stuck

and crushed inside the garbage truck. No one knows what happened before that, and as always happens with newspapers, the real issue was never discussed. But people have eyes, and where the tongues have no place to work, the eyes grow keener. The nosy people notice N.'s mother collects his payment and his insurance money, and his wife silently collects whatever is left of his corpse, only to give him a small burial ceremony. Then, both women pack their things and move away. The misery of the decrepit women floundering away into another shallow hole of poverty as the dead man lay down peacefully in the city cemetery somehow lessens the suffering of the poor souls toiling away their lives, wishing there won't be a next time on this hardened, unforgiving Earth.

They still remember the shadow of the kid, ever so tiny in the hand-me-downs from some sort of Salvation Army reserved for the filthy beggars whose names are never found anywhere except missing reports. He trails after his mother and grandmother, seemingly lost, not knowing if his father would someday return, not understanding that the word "death" means a one-way ticket. He assumes that his father has taken an important role, and the hearse proves the grandiosity of his position. He's too young to realize the pity in the people's eyes, and that the grandiosity of the black hearse comes too early for a person at his father's age. The cruelty of innocence is the pain comes too late, and its interests accumulate with the years. But the kid doesn't want to hear this. He wants to stay. He wants to wait for his father to be back.

Perhaps the kid will soon forget all of this, when he settles with his mom and grandmother in another manual-labor town. But the women's stories belong to the future, and the lives of the drunken husbands are always too busy for them to care about the next chapter in a sorry tale. After all, no one stays in the past and nothing lives in the future. And in a matter of days, the people erase their existence from the earth. They might be living somewhere else, but not here. Not where the money doesn't grow on trees and the people always have their heads down, counting their steps, busying their hands, dirtying their whole bodies in heaps of garbage, digging deeper and deeper, trying to find in that pile of waste a way to their future.

"But that was no way to die at all," the journalist says to the old garbage collector who worked the same shift with N. She is the only one who still follows the story when everyone else has moved on after the day the last fistful of earth was thrown on N.'s grave.

"Well, what d'ya wanna know? He's done time with life. Now he's down there doing time with death." The man chews a toothpick. "Either way, the poor bastard lived a poor bastard's life and died a poor bastard's way."

"What happened before that? Was he... Was he depressed? Was it suicide? What did the company say?"

"What the hell's 'depressed'?" the old man asks curtly, squinting his eyes against the glare of the sunlight. "An' why woulda sonabitch choose death when he can choose to live on? Is that bitch 'depressed' that strong that she forces 'im to kill 'imself?"

"I don't know. Perhaps he was just...just too sad to live." The journalist is at a loss for words. She looks up, wanting to explain how depression works and what mental illnesses are, but staring back at her are a pair of glazed eyes, red at the rims, on a dark, mottled face. The wrinkles fold into each other, making the man's face look like a testament to life's greater suffering. So great that the meaning of "depression" is but a spoonful of salt dropping into an ocean.

"You fuckin' stupid bourgeoisies with your fuckin' stupid bourgeoisie idears. 'Too sad to live,' eh? And what can death do about it? The only thing it can do is to bring more sadness. Listen here, missum, have you seen his wife and mother?" The man scoffs, shifting his legs.

"I haven't had the chance, and nobody told me their address. I hear that they moved somewhere far away."

"Then you haven't seen pain yet," the old man cackles. "'Too sad to live.' You younguns are real fancy. Listen here, missum, when you live to my age, you know that the saddest thing in life is knowing that living is pain but you must—*must*—go on living anyway. You younguns must have it real good that you think you can choose death."

"So was it suicide?" the journalist persists.

"Who cares? The sonabitch died. What use would it do to dig 'im up and relive the pain over and over again?"

"I just can't fathom it." She scribbles in the notebook. "How can one man jump straight into the garbage truck and get torn into pieces and—I don't understand—not feel anything? Did anyone hear him scream? What was it like in his final moment? What did he think before he made the jump? You were there. Why wouldn't you stop him? Why?"

"Missum, listen," the old man tuts, holding a finger in front of her to shut her up, "I ain't gonna take responsibility for nothing I didn't do. I was there, alright. But I ain't paid to watch over toddlers. I was picking up trash. He's a grown man. If he wanted that one-way ticket, he'd be free to go thataway. You think I have it easy?"

"No, I just…" the journalist stutters, completely out of her comfort zone, wishing she didn't care so much, wanting to care some more, questioning herself. *Is it wrong to love God's suffering children this much?*

"No one here has it easy. You should know you're real lucky to be idle enough to ask those questions. You're in a privileged position. A position where you can take pity on a man who died, torn to pieces in a garbage truck. I ain't in that position. None of us living in this manual-labor town is in that position. You say 'Why' because you have the power to; we say 'Fuck it' and move on because we don't have nothing left to lose. Look, the sonabitch died. Do you think your questions will bring him back? The train has gone, and you're no God. Even God doesn't want to be God in this dumpster. Now, move."

The journalist sits on the stocky wooden chair opposite the grumpy old man, stunned. The man puts on his worn-out uniform and gets ready for his night shift. *Perhaps I should've let it go,* she thinks. *Everybody tells me to let it go. Why can't I let it go? If only I had a reason,* but she knows that reasons are not what she's looking for. She is yearning for something more. She needs a substance strong enough to make her believe in the living—even just a little bit—to go through another day. She only needs a flame because she is ready to jump, headfirst, at any moment. She looks at the scars on her wrist. The old man's words ring in her ears. *You younguns must have it real good that you think you can choose death.* People are quick to judge when they don't witness the other's pain. And if the roles were reversed, she is not sure she'd not condemn him with the same contempt. They are both dragging their demons with their feet. The old man keeps pushing, while she is losing her steps. And though pain has a universal language, it is not easy to understand.

But she would never choose death for the fun of it. She

would never choose it for a quick way out. There was one time she thought of how nice it would be to not feel the pain of the living world for but a minute. Then the "once" turned into "twice," the "twice" turned into "three times," until the hospital's emergency room became her second home. She never wanted to choose death. She never thought she'd be the kind of quitter who'd choose the quick way out. She doesn't love the feeling of suffocating, the burning sensation in her throat, the teetering step when she hovers between the line of darkness and survival until the light gets in through the cracks of her eyelids.

She was just exhausted from living. And when she heard N.'s story a few months ago, she thought, *Perhaps he was suffering; perhaps I can find the root where it all begins.* There is no cause to her whimsical trip to this manual-labor town. There is no reason for her to tolerate the old man's skeptical cynicism. The women have long gone. What is she here for then? All of a sudden, the tiredness creeps up on her in waves.

"It was no way to die at all," she says. Her voice cracks a little but there are no tears. "It was no way to die."

"Sure, missum, it was no way to die, but he died nonetheless, didn't he?"

"Why did he have to suffer? I don't understand. Why do we all have to suffer? You and him and his women and child, and me, and me, and me…"

"Listen, missum." The old man sits down by her side and pats her trembling shoulders. "I'm no God or philosopher, but I think it's because we're all raised to be strong, to be so goddamned strong."

"But I'm not strong," the journalist protests, her voice tremulous. A tinge of bitterness and mounting hatred shines through in the layers of words.

"That's the cause," the man cackles. "No one is built to be that strong. And whoever built this world keeps demanding, more, more, more. And we keep on begging, 'Don't ask for too much of us.' Neither comes out as the winner. And that's the war. That's the goddamned war."

"But what if we win?"

"Missum, if we had the chance to win, the sonabitch would've been alive."

The old man walks with her to the broken gate of the manual-labor town. The eyes of the starving children follow her stuffed bag with a patient hunger. The sheer force can almost tear the thinning fabric, ravaging through the makeup, the tangled-up pens, the different-sized notebooks, to find at the bottom of them all the lone piece of granola bar, half eaten. *Oh God.* She bites her lips. *My wealth is killing me.* She never knew possessing something could also mean shouldering a part of the world's burden. The guilt drips slowly on her neck and under her armpits in big drops because, despite the riches she holds, she does not carry anything strong enough to alleviate the soaring pain in the clear brown eyes of the hungering children. The sight of their bloating stomachs is etched onto her mind, promised to be the nightmare that forever is made of. She turns her head away, thinking that as long as she can't see it with her eyes, the suffering will not be there, will never exist.

The old man sees her to the cab, closes the door, and waves her away like any other journalist who has come and gone to this God-forsaken town for many months. She clutches her bag to her breasts and watches the red brick buildings float by. The starving eyes of God's suffering children follow her to the doorstep of her company. Their dark, bottomless irises stand starkly against the murky yellow background that should have been their whites. If she closes her eyes long enough, she can feel their eyes carve away her flesh slowly until they reach the heart and gouge it out for the children to feast on. *Perhaps this is what N. felt,* she thinks, *and how can one live like that?*

She closes her eyes in the cool, air-conditioned room. The blank document opens on her computer screen but there are no words. She dreams of the garbage truck, of the old man sweeping the stuck trash from the sewer, his bony legs steeped inside filth and ordure up to his knees all his life. And she dreams of N. But instead of his dead body, she sees herself. There, inside the turbine of the garbage truck, lies her corpse, torn apart, lifeless. In the dark, silent hour of the night, on the empty pavement, the old man and N. keep on sweeping and stuffing trash into the garbage truck. Nobody looks inside the garbage truck. Nobody notices her death. Nobody sees her pain as she screams out, crying for help as the blades of the truck tear through her skin, bringing her to the final ending. Outside the windows of the twentieth floor, a robin chirps a piercing song, shattering the haunting, still night. The journalist wakes up, realizing that she is still on this side of the platform, waiting for her train. Life moves on and she will settle in with happiness at last. She closes the laptop, finally letting go of the case. *That is the cause.* The old man's words run on repeat in her mind like a broken record. *No one is built to be that strong.*

She packs her bag, clocks out, and walks briskly to the station. The bus arrives. She steps on and looks outside the half-open windows. A fierce light almost blinds her. In the opposite direction, the garbage truck drives into the darkness.

Lost in Translation: An Essay in Conversation

N*ếu cuộc đời chỉ toàn chuyện xấu xa*
Tại sao cây táo lại nở hoa[1]
T/N: Life is indeed filled with evil deeds, why does the apple tree still blossom?

Vu sits quietly on her chair, contemplating the letters in her hand. She draws up her legs, her eyes staring through nothingness, her chin resting on her knees. She doesn't know what to make of the letters' content. A few of them caress her with tender words. More of them pierce through her heart. One of them picks up the shattering pieces and glues them together again. The tender night outside still goes on.

Vu watches the clouds drifting together, then drifting apart. The letters in her hands are like burning coals on a wintry night. She can feel her nails clawing at the warmth despite the festering scars from the feeble attempts to gouge at the flame that is never hers to hold. What can she say? They are letters from a friend. A lover for two weeks. A stranger for the rest of her life. Three years' worth of letters to tell her that the writer is coming, but it'd be better not to believe in the miracle

---

[1] T/N: If life is indeed full of evil deeds, why does the apple blossom still bloom?

of something as flimsy as hope. She can hear the laughter in the dark, but she has lost the ability to distinguish between evil and goodness. Looking at the moon, she wonders if that person is still out there, walking the dark alleyway, bearing his burden, and yet still finding it in his heart to say that the moon is beautiful. She feels the tears coming, but when she opens her mouth, only a silent cry comes out. She bends over the desk, her hands trembling. A blank letter is there. All she needs is to write a few words and give this pain in her chest a meaning.

A knock on her door draws her back to the room, bare cold with its sparse furniture: a makeshift bed, a table to write, a laptop, a chair, and a shelf full of books. She says, "Come in," knowing that this night will be long, that this won't be the last night, that she shouldn't have invited the person on the other side of the door in from the beginning. That she can live without another person interfering in her life, but the night is maddening with its deafening bellows of wounds and the will to live.

A young girl steps in, closing the door behind her harshly then pacing back and forth. Her name is Ai. She has that name because she was born out of love, but she was raised to be a fighter. She is a storm. A force of chaos in the otherwise peaceful and calm darkness. The two girls have been sharing the same house for many moons. Vu still remembers the first day Ai came to her doorstep with a small backpack and a little suitcase filled to the brim with books. She said, grinning, "I will be disturbing you at night." And disturb Vu she did. Ai hates words without meaning and actions without warning. She is young and tender. Her heart is fierce, but it has yet learned the taste of vengeance and hatred, the seasons that every person needs to feel alive.

Ai glances at the letters in Vu's hand then with a quick movement, throws them in the air. The moon hangs in the sky, showing half of her face, full of beauty, of poignancy that makes Vu stop breathing for a moment. The girl's eyes are glowing, a soft brown color with a transparent film of tears that are never there but can freeze a whole summer. She speaks, her voice firm, her tone showing more anger than curiosity: "Why do you still have these good-for-nothing letters?"

Ai knows the writer, a forsaken soul who had chosen the will to power over the freedom to be true. Ai detests his hunger, saying he will never be satisfied. He is a monster with an insatiable palate. And all this time, Vu keeps giving and giving and giving. Ai simply waits. She wants an ending to something that's already a foregone conclusion. But Vu refuses to believe in something that can be so easily proven. Vu wants fiction.

"I don't know, Ai," Vu says, her eyes hazy. She is not here. She is never here when Ai storms in through the door, pacing the room till morning, throwing the books down, baring her teeth, biting Vu's mind. "I never know. I thought I'd take a walk through the past and find in it a glimpse of truth. But it is not so easy. See, I interpret the past as a person who's still living there, but this person…" Vu catches a letter. "He's already in the future."

"You interpret the past as a choice; he interprets it as a mistake. How can you stop people from hurting each other when they wield their right for freedom but are willingly caught inside power's trap? Stop living on dreams," Ai says, exasperated by Vu's blank face. Living together for this long, Ai knows far too well Vu's tendency to immerse in a realm of fake hope and borrowed happiness. The realm of what could have been. The realm of lies and pretense.

"Why are you here this late in the night? I thought you wouldn't come but once in while," Vu says, changing the subject, swirling her chair around, taking a book from the shelf. A book in a foreign language. To Vu, any language is foreign. She doesn't speak their hypocrisy, and she never understands the victory with which they so forcefully grab her throat, choking her, molding her, until she is one of their own. A piece of a human, lost in translation. Her tongue burns with the desire to be understood, but the stream of people keep passing her by, listening to her cry, and interpreting that as the pitiful sound of a soldier on the way home after a losing battle, with his comrade's corpse on his shoulders. And it is true. Vu has a dead comrade on her shoulders. He is called Memory.

But somehow, Vu understands Ai's language. The language of feelings, of emotions, of a heart full of dreams and a mind stuck inside a body too little to make the earth move but too large to fit inside a society filled with boxes and frames. Ai herself is a foreign language no one wants to learn. The price is too steep and the benefit they can reap from it is nothing but blood. Vu watches Ai with absolute admiration as the girl stands there in the moonlight, her eyes unwavering, her lips tight. The fire for the living is burning so bright inside her that she doesn't need a sun to show her the way. Vu repeats her question, her feet slowly touching the ground of her reality. "Why are you here? Something tickle your mind?"

"I read a book about war."

"Which war?"

"Guess."

"I don't know." Vu smiles bitterly, her face resting on her arm as she curls up in her chair and leans on the tabletop. Her eyes are sparkling, reflecting the silvery light of the moon and the starry sky. "The earth's existence is the existence of war. See, our history is filled with so many wars that everyone thinks we won peace over. But when you look at the earth from the moon, you can still see the flaming tongue of the war gods and goddesses licking through the burning cities. We never learn."

"But this war is different."

"How so?"

"Because it speaks my language."

Vu looks deep into Ai's eyes. She stops laughing; her hands curl into a fist, grasping at thin air. "Ai," she says, not knowing whether it is a condolence for her or a reprimand for Ai, "war doesn't have a language."

Ai doesn't seem to pay any attention to her words. Even if she heard the sentence, Vu doubts Ai will show any sign of conceding. She demands truth for truth's sake. She yanks truth from the hands of whichever side claims to possess it and dissects it to the last punctuation. But Vu is different. She demands lies for peace's sake. After all, no matter how hard she fights for the truth, the only thing she can protect is her world—this room full of books and a bed full of dreams. Perhaps the truth never matters as much to her as it does to Ai. She often imagines in her wildest nightmares that truth is a silent ghost looming there at the foot of her bed, ten feet tall, with a double row of teeth, eating at her heart, enjoying her pain, and demanding her flesh and blood. The truth wants her bones. She once waged war against a friend, hoping truth would defend the intangible fence of the already-toppling castle. But at the end of the final battle, truth gouged out her heart, pointing to the people leaving and the people dying, bleeding for their version of victory, telling her what was obvious from the start: in war, as in all things in life, he was the first casualty.

She forces herself to focus on Ai. The girl sits on the edge of her makeshift bed—a mattress with a fleece blanket thrown on top—and looks listlessly at the moon hanging outside the windows. Vu knows that look far too well, and she doubts she will be able to sleep tonight. That look is the permanent signal for the beginning of their debate. And it's tiring, because neither of them debates to win. It is their only means to kill their loneliness. Ai says, "Doesn't it make you wonder?"

"What?"

"You say war doesn't have a language, but yesterday night, when I read that book, I could hear it speak my name."

"How so?"

"It said it had seen my enemy. That I didn't belong to history, and I would never belong. Be it the side of my enemy or the side of my country, I would forever be torn apart, thinking I could use love to defend peace. It said it had killed peace so that people could live with their demons. But Vu, when I asked it, 'What about me?' the war answered, 'I killed you, but you keep on existing.' Vu, what does it mean?"

"I told you, didn't I? War doesn't have a language. It doesn't speak the tongue of the victor. Neither does it tell the tales of the vanquished. It kills and it kills and it kills. In silence, you can hear the battle cry, and only in silence can you hear the soft fall of the dead body. War doesn't have a language because it doesn't need to speak."

"Then why did it speak to me?"

"Maybe inside you, there is a war going on."

"Or maybe out there, where the war is fighting for its throne, it gets tired, and it needs—"

"Love?" Vu snickers with contempt.

"No, pity."

"They are demons of the same tribe."

"Then why are we holding onto them?" Ai shouts, standing up in a rush then falling back to the bed once more. She fumbles with the blanket, her eyes dark with embers like burning coal.

"Because we are living."

"You call this living?" Ai points to the bare room. She picks up the books on the shelf and throws them on the floor, mocking, "You and your precious books in languages you can't speak or understand. What are you so desperately looking for in them? The past that had you cowered in the dark? Or the future who plays you in its palm? Remember, you are forever stuck in the present of a life you don't want to lead. Now tell me this, do you call it living?"

"And who has the right to define what is living?" Vu screams, then with mockery, she cackles at Ai's anger, feeling herself defeated in the wild forest of unknown emotions. Tonight, Ai is different. And perhaps tomorrow, she will be even more different. She is growing, climbing up the slope, carrying the weight of Atlas, waiting for the right time to dump it down the abyss and watch the world burn underneath her feet. Meanwhile, Vu is here, stuck inside the darkening room with a half-written letter and the books she never understands, finding that by tolerating pain, she can feel the beating of her heart before Death comes by to visit her again. How ironic for them to argue about things neither can control. Between the two of them, the living is the dividing line. But Vu refuses to admit that foregone conclusion. With a defeated smile on her tired face, she asks, her hand reaching for a poetry collection on the bookshelf, "Do you know why the apple trees blossom?"

"What?"

"I once read somewhere in between the pages of the books that lay down to rest around my insomniac nightmare— a romantic poet asks the world a seemingly meaningless question. He says, 'If the world is indeed filled with evil, why does the apple tree blossom?' And I've wondered ever since. I care less for the right meaning; rather, I find in it a feeble cry for hope. An illusion, almost, of peace and of what could have become of humans. Don't you ever question it? If the world feasted on wars and the lives of innocent children, if that beast of the ancient calamity can't live without shedding blood to grow the tree of vengeance, then is there goodness on earth? So, I ask you the unheard-of question—the ridiculous notion of something so mundane people don't even pay attention to it—tell me, why do the apple trees blossom?"

Ai is silent. From the wild-eyed look and her flushed cheeks, Vu knows Ai is thinking of something else. Something more intense. Something naïve enough to prove that she is still untainted yet strong enough to fill her with a will to live. Something bad. And Vu welcomes it all. Ai's thoughts are the ideals of a person who still believes that love could save everything. Vu never says that the girl is wrong. She simply opts for a different path. A path less trodden, where no human would cross. The path of life. The path of suffering in the sweetness of knowing that no matter what, the only choice is to walk on. Ai lowers her head, heaves a sigh, and mumbles, "Last night, I dreamed of them dying."

"Who?"

"The people who were killed and the people who killed. After a while, they switched positions. But in the end, what was left of the two sides was a field of bones. The empty eye sockets stared into nothingness. That is where we belong. We are born from nothingness, and we will return to its cold embrace once again. And I wonder, why does that fact not make us a race full of love? The poet was right to ask his question. Who knows why the apple trees blossom?" Ai laughs sarcastically. She swipes the pile of books on Vu's bed to the ground, assumes her seat on the soft pillows, and leans on the wooden headboard. "I think your poet is the only one who cares."

"Perhaps. But don't you find hope in it?" Vu says, turning back to her letters. She languidly flips through each of them, catching words and losing their meanings.

"I find desperation."

"So you think that poet is asking for help."

"I think he's trying to egg himself on. To make himself believe that there is love after all. That to believe in goodness is goodness itself," Ai says, rocking herself back and forth, making the bed creak under her weight.

"Then what about evil?"

"I think he believes in evil. It's just—" Ai lifts her head, staring at Vu with the same poignant eyes. The transparent brown irises reflect the moonlight, and Vu can see the world swim in them. Ai speaks with a firm voice, "It's just a matter of the old wisdom. To be or not to be. If you believe in evil, there's no place for goodness. But if you believe in goodness, then evil has won. You already know how much depends upon the tip of the scale in your conscience. If you can't see the blossom, what is left for you to choose but to believe in a world that will continuously be at war until the last remnant of our civilization is reduced to a single rock? To bloom or not to bloom. Do you think you have an option?"

"I think we have options. Far too many of them. But Ai, you put your bet in the extremes. I'd rather stand on the sidelines and watch," Vu speaks rather curtly. She doesn't want to involve herself in Ai's wrecked philosophy. She doesn't want sympathy for a race that can foster something as wicked as betrayal and as tender as hope. Rather, she wants to detest it. But she has failed. After all, none have succeeded.

"You'd rather watch the earth crumble?" Ai retorts. There's no laughter or happiness in her voice.

"Watch the last men kill each other until there's no humans left and yet, they'd still call it justice."

Vu chuckles but Ai remains immovable. It doesn't matter. Vu knows Ai doesn't take offense at her deprecating humor. Ai understands Vu far too well to feel anger for the girl's off-beat response to anything she says. And in that way, the room gets warmer for a fraction of a second.

"Do you believe that the apple trees will blossom even when people are raining bombs on them?" Ai mocks.

"I don't know. Do you ever see a soldier stopping his machine gun in front of a civilian woman?" Vu replies, ignoring the daggers in Ai's words. She is hurt, but more than that, she doesn't want to admit that she is going to lose the final battle within her. Ai is right. To hope or to be hoped for: does Vu ever stand a chance in the choice she makes?

"I haven't. But I have seen soldiers shooting themselves to stop the war from stealing the last piece of their humanity," Ai says contemplatively.

"Because the rest of their humanity is used to massacre and to maim the enemy's humanity."

"In that moment, do you think they understand their conscience?"

"Does that make a difference for the civilians?" Vu punches the table hard. Her face is still smiling but her whole body is tensed with an unknown, uncalled-for anger. *God*, she thinks, *Why doesn't this girl stop pushing me to the edge of this abyss?*

"You talk as if you believe the world is filled with evil," Ai huffs, exasperated with Vu's indifferent fury. Vu often says she's given up on life because she never wants to be the one abandoned. But Ai knows Vu still has it in her, or rather, Ai wants to believe that Vu still has it in her to live.

"And you, old enough to be wiser yet young enough to act bolder, you talk as if you believe in goodness," Vu retorts. Slowly, she has become weary of the conversation. She knows Ai is far from satisfied with her lukewarm attitude and their talk may go on until morning. She knows Ai won't let her wallow in what the girl calls pessimism but Vu calls living. She also knows that Ai will stop at nothing to reach a conclusion— an ending of a whimsical journey through the abyss of sleepless nights where they lay there sleeping, listening to the sound of the weeping wind. Outside, the darkness is creeping through the tall condominiums. The windows light up for a fleeting second then fade back into darkness again.

Vu sits on her chair, holding a letter in front of her, reading the few last sentences: *I know you've been waiting for me.* And it's true, she had been waiting for a person who never promised his coming. While Ai is waging chaos after chaos in the night, Vu is silently holding her front of the battle. Why does she still keep these good-for-nothing letters folded neatly on her desk? She doesn't know why herself. Sometimes, in the most desperate moments, when Vu witnesses the silent death of the leaves as the wind carries them to their earthly grave, she almost believes that she possesses the power to change the outcome of something that is already shattered beyond repair. But what does she care? After all, she will never step outside the room. Ai thinks she needs a dose of hope. Vu thinks she needs a dose of love. Neither can heal her wounds, but at least Vu wants to choose the poison that will cause the least pain.

"Hey, what if the apple trees never blossom?" Ai asks absentmindedly, staring at her fingers as she spreads them out in front of her eyes, "What if there's no goodness in the beginning?"

"Then there would be no humanity." Vu tries to smile to lighten the mood, but her chest tightens; her eyes glisten. Her laughter sounds more like a mourner's tears than a happy young woman. She is surprised at how much despair Ai has successfully drawn from her heart in a single night. Looking at the sky, Vu thinks about the morning that will always come, the days that will always progress, and the way the world will keep going on. "I don't know what will be here if there were no goodness in the beginning, but one thing is for sure, if the world is a dark abyss and life is filled with evil deeds, humans wouldn't exist."

"Do you think we feast on goodness?" Ai perks up her head. She twirls her short hair to mimic Vu, but her hair keeps sliding off her fingers. In a flustered moment, she lays her hands down then moves them around the bed, not knowing what to do with them. They are free to hold treasure, and they are also free to destroy it. Suddenly, Ai finds her hands to be stronger than any of her body parts. They are the instrument for the will to power.

"No, I think we feast on the belief that there will be goodness," Vu says absentmindedly, not noticing Ai's frantic hand movements on her bed.

"Then is there goodness after all?"

"That's where the poem comes in: Why does the apple tree

blossom?"

"To prove that there is goodness," Ai says stubbornly.

"No, to prove that evil is there, and even if the apple tree blossoms, what does it matter to the evil? The poet is holding onto something so frivolous, so feeble, so sickeningly bitter in its sweetness: he's hanging onto life through hope."

"You're saying that because you refuse to believe in goodness," Ai mocks. She picks up a letter, reads through it, stops at the phrase, *I only show this place to you and,* then crunches up her nose and crumples it into a ball.

"No, I'm saying that because I detest hope. You'd do better in life without believing in it."

"Then what do you believe in, Vu?" Ai asks. In her frustration, she throws down a row of books. She never gets why Vu must torture herself simply for living. She never understands the reason behind Vu's struggle to climb up the hill no one wants to ascend. The hill of desperation, of hopelessness, of death and decay. By the time she came to know Vu, the girl had already buried half of her life eight feet under. Vu kneels there in the gruesome rain of the future, her face showing a smile of surrender. Ai knows then that no matter what happens, to Vu, the war is over, and she is one of the defeated. Rooming with Vu is like rooming with a twisted mirror. Ai can only see her future fragmented in it, but she can see how her past is creeping up on her until it smothers her in regret and what could have been. Ai repeats the question in self-mockery, "What do we believe in?"

"I wonder…" Vu looks far away into the blue night. The dry tone and the bitterness in her eyes shine on a life that is far too used to the faithless but is still believing in the glimmer of saintly hope. "Either way, I'm still going to live. That's the tragedy."

"I believe in goodness."

"So you believe in the apple trees."

"No," Ai says, looking intently at Vu, her voice strong and firm, "I believe in the world of the poet. A world where there is evil, but we can indulge ourselves in goodness."

"Do you think we as a race are capable of goodness in evil? Look out there," Vu points at the moon. "We walked on the moon while using nuclear technology to destroy. Whether you know about them or not, the wars are still going on. People are dying. People are killing. The corpses are piling on top of each other, building a mountain of justified crimes and unnecessary sacrifices. And can you believe it, as you cradle a newborn to your bosom, the moon is shining its shivering beauty upon the dead and the blood-soaked battle? Do you think that it's goodness still? Or is it evil?"

"Then why are we going to war?" Ai shouts. Her chest is palpitating. She finds it hard to breathe. In her mind, she repeats a thousand times the phrase, *Don't destroy my last bit of hope.* And Vu can see her pleading eyes. Vu smiles gently, stroking Ai's soft hair.

"Because we believe we are right, and we are protecting what is right."

"But—"

"But the other side also believes that they are right, and they'll also protect what is right to them," Vu says, half laughing in her usual sarcastic tone whenever this subject is broached. "There is no war to end all wars. See, you are tiptoeing on a very thin line between your ideals and what is real. Tell me, Ai, after reading that book of war, do you still think that humans can be contained within good and evil? That we are either good or evil? No, we are beyond those definitions. So no, Ai, wars don't speak your language. Wars are pieces of foreign languages pierced together by the death toll of all sides, and the war stories they tell will depend on how you interpret the various languages involved. Perhaps somewhere along the road, you will find that the meaning behind all those wars of attrition is long lost in translation. After all, what are we dying for if not the chance to sing the last song of freedom and the first verse of hope? That, at least, is how I think of the apple trees. Let them blossom so we can believe."

"And do you believe?"

"If given the freedom of choice," Vu says, turning her gaze to Ai. Her eyes sparkle ever so slightly to reflect the ring of moonlight. "I will choose to believe. But life has led me through many twists and turns, and when I look back at the road I've traversed, all I find are the stories of someone else. Someone who's no longer me. Someone who has killed herself so I could live. We must grow, I agree. But witnessing the arduous path, strewn with the empty corpses of the people who had chosen to move on before me, I sometimes wonder, is it worth it? After learning about war, do you choose to believe? And believe in what?"

"Vu, without belief, you can't survive a winter," Ai says, lying down on the makeshift bed. She throws the blanket on, snuggling into the warm nest, questioning Vu. "If you choose to believe, you must believe in goodness."

"There was an old wise man who said that people are born with innate goodness."

"And you don't believe him?"

"I think he shares the same view as the poet. They believe in the little miracle called life. I wish I could learn to see the beauty

40

of their world," Vu says, picking up a pen. The scratching of her pen on the fine letter paper lulls Ai like sweet music to an aching soul, tempestuous but always looking for a healing miracle.

"But you're already seeing the beauty of their world," Ai yawns. Dawn is drawing near.

"What makes you think so?"

"Because you're still holding onto the letters."

"It doesn't make me a believer."

"But it makes you hope. And you said hope was the cruelest thing, yet the most beautiful thing, in the world."

"I did say that, didn't I? Because I was naive," Vu says. Her voice grows smaller and smaller until it becomes a soft whisper, blowing in the wind. "I should've never trusted the word of a person who's leaving. I thought my world was big enough to give him freedom. But what he was seeking was chains and prison. He needs the walls to feel safe. I need the sky to stay alive. We said the word 'love,' but to each of us, it meant different things. If the Tower of Babel hadn't fallen, perhaps there would be less pain when we were parting. The next time we meet—but there will be no next time for something that's buried in the past, will there?"

"Even so," Ai says, turning on her side, watching Vu's figure as she curls up on the chair, one hand holding a letter, the other holding a pen in midair. Her eyes stare through the words without comprehending their meaning. Ai quietly repeats, letting the words fall softly on Vu's pain, "Even so, what will you lose to hope and to believe in love again?"

"I don't know. And that's what makes it scary."

"The soldier in the war story..." Ai changes the topic, seemingly not listening to Vu's weak groan of protest. The night is getting long, and Vu wants her bed back. But Ai is not the type to leave until the storm has passed its peak. "He said that he killed because at that time he believed it was right to do so. But don't you find it strange? A human, killing another human, who has the same shape, the same bones, the same figure as him, because he believes it is right. We convince ourselves that the other side is not human so we can ease our conscience. But what about the aftermath? When the war ends—let's suppose there's an end—and the soldier goes back to his home, will he not look at his fellow citizens and be reminded constantly that he had killed an enemy who was exactly the same as him? How do we live after that?"

"We don't live, Ai. The soldier—me, you, or anyone and everyone—we don't live. We shed our skins and move on, thinking we could be a new person. People are all broken. We indulge in evil, yet we believe in salvation. In goodness. In a world where we can understand one another. In the name of that belief, we wage war after war and after losing the battle, we wage war on peace. I don't think I've ever lived, Ai. I think I'm shedding my old skin, thinking that the new one will be less painful to move inside. What about you? Have you ever lived?"

Ai closes her eyes. Her face is tranquil. She looks like she's sleeping on the question, taking Vu's pessimism as the sweetest, honey-covered pills and chewing them until they grow bitter again. "I've lived," she finally says. "I don't know if I've ever shed my skin. I know I've been broken. Some parts of my body shine with scars; other parts are still bleeding. But I love the pain. Only then can I know that I'm living to my full extent. Vu, do you think that your life will forever be buried underneath all those letters and the words that you

42

don't understand? What are you trying to achieve, unlearning the tongues you're speaking?"

"I gave up on living. I chose surviving. And maybe that's why we're having this conversation tonight. I brought it upon myself by keeping these letters and by reading too much. You're right. I'm a hypocrite." Vu smiles, turning around to face Ai's eyes. The transparent brown is still there, and the moon is ever so beautiful, shining on Ai's wavy hair. Vu feels like she is immersed in an ocean of hurt. Her pain is caressed but it is not healed. "I unlearn the language so I can refuse hope. But look at me, every word I say carries a glimmer of hope. Because I can't cease the ride of existence, I learn to cohabitate with hope. I don't want to see the beauty of the apple trees' blossom, but Ai, how I yearn for it. How each of us yearn for it. I guess that's what the poet wants to say."

"Hm hm," Ai mumbles, rubbing her eyes, turning to face the wall. Vu knows that tonight will end like so many nights before and so many nights after. That Ai will fall asleep on her bed and let her feel the warmth of another person for a fleeting second, only to disappear suddenly at the first ray of the morning sun. She knows there is no book of war. She knows Ai only wants to talk. Looking out the windows, Vu realizes they are the epitome of loneliness. A city full of darkness and their windows are the only thing that's lit up. Ai slurs her words. "Vu, it doesn't matter if the wars were there or not. The apple trees will always blossom. That's why, if given the choice, please always choose to believe in goodness."

"Even if there is evil?"

"Heh, if the world is indeed filled with evil, why does the apple tree blossom?"

The girl falls into a deep sleep. Her snoring calms the burning passion within Vu's heart. She picks up the letters scattered on the floor, finishes writing the current letter, then puts it into a glass bottle. Tomorrow, she will throw the bottle into the open sea. Who knows. Maybe this time around, she can believe in hope.

Because in Vu's name, there is always a storm waiting to rage on, to live, to yearn, to desire for the burning flame. Her name in the English language means chaos, thunder, and lighting. Ai's name, on the other hand, is the epitome of love, of peace, of a belief in all things human, of freedom and roses. But as two lonely humans on sleepless nights, waiting for the sunrise, the meaning of their names is lost in translation. They drag on the debate, day by day, night by night. How can they win a fight with no metrics of victory? Vu never knows. She doesn't bother to. Ai refuses to acknowledge the rules of anything.

They settle for peacemaking, the words exchanged in the heated passion of the living. By tomorrow morning, Ai will wake up, forgetting the whole debate. Vu will continue her life, writing letters to the broken man on the other side of the globe, hoping against hope that he will call. Life always finds a way to move on. And on nights like this, the debate will repeat itself. Ai asked Vu if she called this living. Unbeknownst to Ai's fiery heart, Vu's answer is stone cold, set down with the determination of a woman who has gathered everything within her to walk on water. "Yes," Vu says to herself. "It takes an ocean of hurt for me to learn that as long as the eyes are open, we are living." She looks at the dawning sun. Outside the windows, the apple tree is slowly blossoming. Spring is late in its wake, but it will always be here, hiding beneath the dewdrops on the blossom's frail petals, waiting with fervent patience.

The Lonely Race

"Hey, did you know that people who often take long, hot showers are lonely?"

He sits on the bed by the large windows, watches with silent eyes as the sky pours down tears and pain. The entire human race is reduced to red and yellow neon lights. He turns the pages of the book, not necessarily reading them, but it seems like he can feel their loneliness. It is oozing out from his bony fingers and the blue veins on his thin wrist. His hair covers half of his face. My eternal anguish is not knowing what is in those eyes, so dark with sadness and so unfathomable with fear. Every time I gaze into that darkness, I always think, *Lord, have mercy on me.* But the Lord never has it.

"Did you know that people only take hot showers to mimic the warmth of human skin?"

His finger lingers on the corner of a specific page. I cannot make out the lines and the words, but I don't need to feed my curiosity and peek because as soon as he catches my eyes, he reads out loud:

"Did you really love the city? Or did you just pretend?"

"So it says," I whisper as I lay on my side, hand in his hand, head on his lap.

"So he says," he laughs, turning to another page. "Leonard

Cohen. Never gets old."

Yes, but only with him. We've known each other for five years, lived together for three. I know he hates spicy food, loves the rain, detests the snow. Sometimes, like this night, when the weather is not good enough to go anywhere fun but also not bad enough to lay in bed, waiting for sleep, he'd pick up a coarse philosophical book and ask me questions with no right answers.

He never knew how much I hate Leonard Cohen. The dreary old songs; the hoarse, raspy voice; the mythical lyrics, his preaching about G-d (yes, that's how Cohen wrote his verses, my boyfriend shows me) make me sick unto death.

It's alright, I console myself, rubbing his kneecap. He never asks me to remember every little thing. I love him all on my own.

"So did you really love the city?" I fiddle with his fingers, twist them, bring them closer to my lips, and place butterfly kisses on his fingertips. "Did you?" I turn my eyes up to catch his in a sweet embrace.

"Do you think I did?" He leans in closer, and I can smell the powdery fragrance on his hair. "Or do you think I just pretend?"

"No one can pretend that long."

"Really? No one?"

"No one."

"Ever?"

"Ever."

He chuckles, a soft, tinkling sound in his voice. The sound rings in my ears like silver spoons clinking on glasses. My heart sinks to the bottom of hell and I stop living for one second. The words stick into my flesh like needles, threading into my existence like thistles and weeds. Pretend. Ever. He never loves anyone but himself. Why do I still hold onto this flimsy relationship that started out as a one-night-stand?

People think the longer you are together, the deeper the love grows. It is the greatest misconception. The number of years just show that you've become better at tolerating each other. Like a punishment dressed in a fancy suit and tie.

Putting the boring book on the nightstand, he lights a cigarette, puffs a few times, and watches the smoke swirl into the thick, rainy night air. The ember glows in the dark, but neither of us feel the warmth. He asks, out of nowhere at all: "Honey, do you know the lonely race?"

"The lonely race?"

"The race where people are soft-boiled eggs with scars and bruises all over. You gather them up and they are just a heap of longing and solitude. A beautiful mess. Bleeding and living. The race where people take long, hot showers because they want to feel the warmth of human skin."

"And are you a part of that race?" I smirk. Between the two of us, it is hard to determine which one is lonelier than the other, which one is human, and which one belongs to that lonely race of his.

"That depends. Are you?"

He leaves a soft kiss on my forehead as I look at him, bewildered and held hostage by his beauty. Relentlessly hurt by his sadness. Captivated by his firm profile reflected on the windows, wondering if he, too, would disappear when the first step of spring comes by. And at that singular moment, amidst the thousand molecules and evolutions within billions and billions of years, I get a painful premonition that no matter how much I try, he will never fall in love with the city. No one ever will.

Holding onto hope because without hope, we will start doubting the gift handed to us by the good Lord above, the priest preached to us in the previous Sunday morning mass. Maybe that's what I'm doing now. If I love him more than whatever will remains of our existence by the end of time, will he love me back?

"I want a kiss." He plays with my fingers the way a lazy cat would. His eyes stare fixedly at the page. The neon signs underneath keep flashing, crying out for the solitude of humanity because the human race has lost the ability to understand each other's suffering since the Tower of Babel was built on land where it didn't belong.

Opposite us, a window silently lights up. Someone just returned home from a long trip. Perhaps they will take a long, hot, steamy shower. They belong to the lonely race, and all the lonely race wants from God is a human's embrace. But as cruel and inhuman as gods are, they only grant to the lonely race a hot shower.

"I want a kiss."

"You're persistent."

"I'm not persistent. I long for it." It is true. The longing for the thing we couldn't have will outlive us. He wants someone to fill the night. I want permanence. We are crossing paths briefly, and I have no way of knowing when he will depart for his next journey.

"Longing for or a kiss? That's silly."

"Plenty of people do silly things for a kiss."

"Like who?"

"Romeo and Juliet."

"That's purely fictional." He exhales a ring of smoke, letting the ember flicker in the somber bedroom.

"Like the Berlin Wall. Like the peace at the end of every World War. Like the plague. I could go on." I shrug, purring as his hand runs through my hair.

"Don't. It just makes us more pathetic."

"Us? You mean you and me?"

"No. The lonely race. Knowing from where and whence we will end, we should've loved each other more. Yet," he gestures vaguely around the room, "here we all are."

"And you hate that fact enough to refuse me a kiss?" I snicker, mocking his avant-garde philosophy, because I know it's true. Because there's no helping people change. Because what doesn't kill us, doesn't kill us. Because the conversation is getting too sad for me to indulge his whims any further.

He smiles sweetly and shakes my fingers off, with no force at all. He knows I won't let go, and because he knows it so well, he is always the one to let go first. I watch as his hair falls. His eyelashes spread into a thin, quivering black veil, half hiding his black-jewel eyes, half hiding the empty void of his existence. I am no believer, and he is no godly being who needs to be worshiped. But in that split second, when he tucks his hair mindlessly away, when the long eyelashes dance gently under the shadow of the moonlight, I pray that God will have mercy on me and throw my whole existence into his warm bosom.

"Me, I long for love and light. But must it come so cruel, must it come so bright?"

"Isn't that a Leonard Cohen song?"

"You know I only listen to Leonard Cohen nowadays."

"Well, maybe it's time you switch it up," I offer, hoping he will stop putting on those dreadful records that sound more like a hearse's wheels rolling over cobblestones.

"To what?" he replies. His eyes are glinting provocatively.

"I don't know—to something that would make you happier?"

"But I don't feel sad." There he goes. I roll my eyes. Of course, he will make things difficult for me. That's his sole joy in this relationship.

"Not feeling sad does not equal happiness." I patiently play along.

"And you think you'd know that?"

"I know." I stroke his hair and find an escape route to the black jewels that pull me in and lean in closer, my forehead to his. "I always know."

I place gentle kisses on his lips, the next one with a stronger force than the last. I want to get to that deepest part of his soul. I want to cross the River Styx and bring him a human heart. I want to see it beating in my hands and forever protect it before the thunder and roars of the ancient gods. I want to ask his soul whether he is a part of the lonely race and whether the lonely race is incapable of love.

His smile returns the loving kisses peppered down the pale white skin. As a smile is not what I am looking for, I keep on pushing. He pulls away, laughing. His hands form a barricade in front of his chest; his hair falls on the pillow as he slips from my embrace. The dark galaxy on a rainy day, with no stars of hope and no stars of existence. I think, *If there were ever a mark to identify the lonely race, this must be it*. I catch him by the waist, then pull him slowly back to my chest. He punches jokingly at me with one hand, his book in the other. He pushes me back and, finally coming to the realization that I am not in any mood to joke, he looks up. Those black jewels will be the end of me. They remind me too much of my mom's black porcelain bowls in the rain. I can still see the raindrops glistening on the edge of the bowls, reflecting the darkness of the hard porcelain and the rainbow. A magical creation.

"Okay, fine, a kiss. Is that what you want?" He smiles gently, and with the bewitching beauty that Hyacinthus once used to entice Apollo in warm embraces and cherry wine, he bestows a kiss on my lips. His breath falls on my face. His hair tickles my skin. I can taste his peach-flavored lip balm and at once, I am reminded of the reason I love the taste of ripening peaches.

I inhale and bury my head in his neck. A faint smell of cardamom and burnt cedar wood overwhelms me, and I can't help but think that this is what I had longed for all those billions of years ago when I was one of the first humans to walk on this immense living ball of loneliness. Now I can see why people love staying in the hot shower. I, too, never want to leave this warmth. I can feel the thin layer of skin quiver under my lips and the pulse of his vein palpitates to celebrate the mortals' existence. With each pulse, I lay down a kiss. He is no longer laughing and his heavy breathing teeters on my mind like a wolf's fangs. I collapse on his chest; my head lies on his heart. He strokes my hair in a slow and mindless motion as if he is still contemplating what all of that was about. I count the lights on the windows opposite me. A lot of people are coming home. The life 20 stories below is ever bustling. I trace back the road that all of the human race has walked to find the origin of the lonely race. I find myself sitting in a cave, billions of years ago, staring at the little shining dots in the sky, none shining for me.

"Why are you crying?"

"Because the stars are dying."

"But that's the whole point. People only see their beauty

when they're dying," he says. "That's the origin of the lonely race."

And as the stars keep on shining, the lonely race will keep on surviving. Because love is powerful, but it can't cure the cruel curse of solitude that all humans are born with.

How to Break Your Heart in Another Language

"Look at it this way. You went on a date with him, and he specifically said he had a girlfriend, and you sat there for two fucking hours, listening to him explaining himself to death—either your death or his death, you don't know, because you stopped listening after knowing that he had a girlfriend—wondering, *Oh gosh, why wouldn't I be better at picking a love interest that resembles love a little more than zero?* You looked at the time and it was already past your lunch appointment, wondering, *Why am I still sitting here?* saying, 'Oh, that must be nice,' in a language you neither know sufficiently nor understand enough to express anything in other than polite and faked kindness. From the gleam in his eyes, you knew he was charmed by your mask, and from the smile on his face, you knew you were doomed. And you repeated time and time again to him, 'Oh, that must be nice,' thinking, *If I understood him clearly, he was talking about how he met his girlfriend,* thinking, *Why is he telling me all of this when he specifically said in his bio that he's looking for something more?* thinking, *Why must it always be me?* thinking, *Why did he want to hurt me this way?* But weren't you the one who wanted to be hurt? You always wanted to be hurt in different languages. Remember the last time you talked to a guy whose native language whispered in the canal of your ears and filled them up and up and up until his words turned into tears on your face? And all the while, you kept thinking, *Not anymore.* You torture yourself with persistence, *Just one more taste.* When they leave you, again, the question rings in your ears like a fucking curse of old. *In how many languages can I spell the words 'idiot' and 'stupid' and 'love' without letting them confuse me?* Am I right?"

"But what if he loves me back?"

"But what if he loves you back? Of course, you must be thinking about that question until it blows your brain into tiny pieces in rose-colored, heart-shaped cells when you invite him for a second date. You typed in a language you didn't know and perhaps no longer have the chance to know, thinking, *I hope he'd agree*, wording your phrase, 'How are you these days?' and all those phony words because you never dared to be hated, learning his language because you were not satisfied to be hurt once, twice, but thrice, in another language. And he agreed, despite knowing that all he wanted from you was an exotic female body from an exotic country where he would never leave behind another footstep after his time was up. So, you picked out a nice dress, put on a thinly veiled mask, a light lipstick. Talking about lipstick, when have you ever liked a light lipstick? And you kept hoping, hoping, hoping, *Please let him choose me*, and losing, losing, losing yourself in a make-believe world, a dreamless void, and you know, you already know, one more step and you will fall off the edge. The vortex had already caught you; too bad. You didn't think you would be sad and desperate and fucked up in another person's bed. And you still don't believe it. After all, you think it's only human to be nice, and give you another million years, you will never think that it is not a human duty to be kind, to be gentle, to know more than breaking the heart of a person. Cruel, I agree, but haven't you read about people in history? Were you not prepared for this story since the day you were born? It is not a 'to be or not to be' question. It has always been a 'to kill or not to kill' question. Why would you let that happen?"

"I don't know. I just thought it would be different."

The windows on the opposite building are gradually lit up. The yellow lights reflect off the walls, shine down on the asphalt street, and finally, jump down the sewer because lights like nothing better than to entwine their bodies with darkness until they are swallowed whole. After all, without darkness, there will be no light. Codependency? No, pathetically designed by nature. The people passing by under the windowsills move up and out of the picture, leaving only shadows and tiny echoes of laughter. The trees rustle and their leaves are murmuring between themselves, speaking in tongues, laughing in tongues, mocking the human race in tongues. But how come they are not falling through the cracks of the windows to leave an opening for the hope of something? The question was never "to be or not to be?" Perhaps, from the beginning, he means, "to survive or to die?"

People choose to be warriors because they think they can fight against the world. Of course, a great man said once that the world breaks people and some will stand up at the broken places. He leaves out the part about those who will not. The bed is getting cold; the down blanket is getting thin. But the girl on the chair refuses to go home, and the girl on the bed refuses to reply with any other sentences than a vague "I don't know." The girl on the bed looks at the bouquet of O'Hara roses, thinking, *I never thought they were named after that O'Hara*, wondering, *Is it true that we are born to hurt and be hurt in return?* saying, "I guess that's just how things are."

"But that's not how things are. That was your choice. You chose to be trampled. You chose to lay yourself down so love could have the chance to grow. But fuck love and that old damn bitch called Fate. If it were love, he'd be with you today, talking about dinners and whatnot. Don't you think he'd have known—he should have known—that it'd be wrong to sow hope on infertile soil? For two hours, he was there, sitting opposite you on a fake old wooden table, thinking, *I could play this game with her until we find out who will be the loser*, thinking, *I'd much prefer a person from my own country*, thinking, *How long is she going to obstruct me and my peace?* Saying, 'I don't have many friends here,' wishing, *If I were lucky, she'd have been in my bed a month ago*. And yet, you believed him. You believed the son of a bitch that you inherently knew from the well-cared-for fingers that he would be no different from the other sons of bitches who sweet-talked you into betraying the only thing of value within you—your country. I wish I could spell out the stupidity in that conversation, highlight it, and scribble notes all over the pages until you can get a single farthing into your head that he will not—ergo, will never—love you back. Why do you let the demons haunt you?"

"Perhaps because the angels are no better. Perhaps because neither of them is the option. I am the option. It's always been that way."

"And you still believe in heaven?"

"I believe in humans."

The girl on the chair whips out a cigarette, lights it up, and puffs on it to see the smoke swirling in the air. Neither of them says anything but both of them understand. The girl on the bed falls back and burrows her head in the pillow, thinking, *If he invites me to dinner*, thinking, *I bet he's way sweeter with his girlfriend. They speak the same language*, thinking, *I want to touch his fingers, feel the tenderness that was meant for her, feel the warmth that was meant for another, feel the skin, feel the curling of the knuckles as they intertwine with mine. I can see his smile, shy and timid, but just see how he thrusts the knife into my vital points, the way he kills, the way he shines with blood on his palms without a guilty look on his lips*, thinking, *I'm falling, falling, falling*.

"And he sat there after you left?" the girl on the chair asked.

"I don't know. What other business does he have with me?"

"You let him in."

"I let myself be an option amongst the sea of options. That's all."

"You let him in, you let him win, you let yourself be Atlas and he was the world."

"He still is the world."

"Haven't you learned from the last time Atlas shrugged?"

"Fuck Atlas. I'd rather be dead than be Atlas."

"But you don't think so. You only need him to be there from the moment you step inside and boom—you're already Atlas."

"I'd rather be dead."

"Do you still believe that you're alive?"

"I'd rather be Sisyphus."

"You'd rather be nothing. You are already nothing. No one is going to be anything. If death is worth that much, why would we still be here, living?"

"I'd rather be in an asylum."

"People don't take lovesick people into the asylum."

"Then who do they take?"

"Insane humans."

"What do you know about insane humans?"

"That they want to be dead."

"But I said I'd rather be dead."

"You'd rather be dead because you have options. Insane humans know they have no option. See, all of us reach the same ending, but the insane humans know they can choose their own ending. That's why they're in the asylum. Choosing your own way out, that's addicting."

"So you are insane?"

"No, I'm nothing. Same as you. Same as everybody else. I'll remain nothing until there are enough of us to move the earth and the wheel of history deems us worthy enough of a name."

The window lights on the opposite building flicker on the asphalt street like a dying flame. A voice is whispering through the leaves. It says, "Kill the flame, kill the flame, kill the flame." But how can one kill the flame when one hardly has it in the beginning? The girl on the bed twists her fingers around the cup's handle, thinking, *God knows how I want her to go*, thinking, *But what else do I have? Who else do I have?* thinking, *Must one kill the flame? Why? What did the flame ever do?* saying, "I think you should leave."

"Must I, then?"

"Suit yourself."

"See, you say I should leave. Why 'should'? If you had said I must leave, then leave I must, alright?"

"You're not talking sense."

"Honey, neither of us are talking sense. None of this makes sense. And tomorrow of tomorrows, no one will ever find out what makes sense and what does not. Why the fuck do you care? Making sense, such a joke."

"You just haven't had enough of my suffering yet."

"Why do you think so?"

"Because you're addicted to my pain. The taste of it just makes you wild, doesn't it? It's exhilarating to walk on glass, and it brings the same sort of exhilaration when you step on the pain of another."

The girl on the chair puffs her cigarette. Not her last, not her first. Around her, on the table, are a dozen unopened cigarette packs, and the empty ones are scattered on the floor. She has been here since this evening, but it feels like she has been here since long before. Longer than the first step of a human on earth, and certainly she will be here until the last human dies on earth. She sits there, thinking, *This stuff is funny. How can she let herself be this pitiful?* thinking, *I really must go home. I don't even know how else I can make it more insufferable both for her and for me,* wondering, *God only knows how painful it is to be living, and that's why He's up there, looking down on us, thinking always that He's the lucky one,* wondering, *What if all the what-ifs become reality?* saying, "God, look at the time."

The girl on the bed does not answer. She tucks her hair behind her ears, drinks cold coffee, leans on the pillow, and looks at the ceiling. Her body's curves show through the sleeping dress. All the feminity within her shows through the half hidden, half revealing outfit. The silk slips on her skin like water dripping down leaves. If the girl on the chair stays silent, she can almost hear the water falling, falling, falling on her eardrums like the sound of a lullaby she had heard sometime long ago. A few lovesick fools had died so the young ones could grow. A few others, stronger lovelorn lovers in the night had chosen to stand up at the broken places so the ones who had fallen could fertilize the earth. No life is too precious to lose, and none is too trivial to leave behind, broken and forsaken though they might be. The girl on the bed thinks of the guy she met yesterday, then the guy she met three years ago, then the guy she met long before she had even known the deceptively sweet taste of betrayal. After all, how cheap is the phrase "I love you?" She reckons if she said it one, two, three thousand times, the phrase would be dead, too.

From the bed, she says, "You can leave if it's too late," thinking, *What else do I have left if she leaves?* thinking, *I could make do if she stays here a bit longer. I bet I could learn to love her the way she loves my suffering,* wondering, *Should I let her stay? After all is through, she will be just another stranger,* thinking, *Whatever. I can still see her on the bus platform or some other place,* thinking, *If I stay quiet, I can hear her footsteps echo from the asphalt street leading to her shelter, and the storm never gets worse nor better,* saying, "Perhaps you could stay."

"To do what? To hurt you in another language?"

"What does it matter? But that's not what I mean."

"Then what do you mean?"

"I just don't want you to be another stranger."

The light is off, one window after another. But inside the apartment on the corner, the cigarette light keeps flaring up one hour to the next. The leaves are silent and the sky is dark. The storm is brewing. From the east, the light is crawling out of its cave like some sort of creepy insect trying to hang onto a single opportunity to live. From the west, the ominous wind blows raging anger. Leaves upon leaves are falling, taking hiding places on the dampened earth. The rain of yesterday has not disappeared yet. Its footsteps and its breath still linger in the hanging branches, under the shadows of the carved balcony. If you were desperate enough, you would think that the scene is almost beautiful. But the girl on the chair is nowhere near the faintest definition of the word *desperate*. She snuffs her cigarette, saying, "I'm going," thinking, *God knows I'll come back here whenever she's calling*, thinking, *If God had known how hard it is to live, why must He make humans a lonely race?* looking at the dawning sky, thinking, *The stars are all dead*, saying, awkward and somewhat embarrassed by the whole mess she's gotten herself into, "Do you want me to stay?"

The girl on the bed puts the cold coffee cup on the nightstand, turns down the shaded lamp, and burrows her head into the pillow. "Who knows. I'm too tired for that." But when she hears the doorknob turn and the faltering footsteps fade away, she sits up on her bed again, looking wildly about in the darkened room, thinking, *You say you don't know but you're hurting me again, and this is not even another language.*

The storm growls. The windows tremble under the weight of the millions of lives before and the millions of lives after. This is not a story. This is just how a person hurts the girl in another language.

I Wish There Was a Treaty

"Hey, have you ever thought about dying?"

There he goes spouting all the nonsensical shit that, through a miraculous gate, always gets from his brain to his mouth at my most inconvenient moment. We tangle ourselves on the soft memory foam mattress, hoping it will retain the memory of us, knowing we are losing this moment to the passage of time. The nightshade turns a deep, warm yellow, and instead of being comforting, it is eerie, bringing with it an uncanny sense of dark premonition. What is real and what is only imaginary? I don't know anymore. Outside, the cars pass by on rare occasion. It is midnight. The stars shine through the open windows, letting us know we should hope, despite the truth that they are all dead. The wind billows in the room, gentle and lulling with the fresh scent of lilies. A mother is telling her child to turn down the light.

I breathe in the familiar scent of ripened peach and berry, immersing myself in the land of what could be if I just let his question go without answering. Instead, I lie on top of him, stunned. My face pauses midair. My lips still pout forward, leaning for another kiss on his warm chest. My eyes stare at him, probably not with a wise man's insight, but with a fool's ignorant frustration. I look down at his face and the lips that know far too well how to kindle a fire of desire and anger at the same time within my weary heart. Oh, why do the fairy tales trick me into believing that the beauty will love the beast?

"I sometimes wonder if you can read the most basic situations," I say. My anger escapes through the barrier of clenched teeth and faked smile.

"Like what?" he asks, feigning innocence, or maybe he believes in his innocence enough to forget that he has sinned for far too long to fit into that godforsaken category. Damn him and the system that creates the meaning of the word *misery*.

"Like now," I say, planting soft kisses down his collarbone, trying to pull him down from wherever he is. Perhaps he is higher than the Empire State Building with the amount of Xanax he chugs down every evening. *Pathetic fools*, I think, *both of us*.

"That so?" He pushes my shoulders and settles my whole body down on the other pillow with a simple maneuver. His fingers dance on my unshaven beard, tickling my face and churning the desire within me.

I watch his nimble fingers draw meaningless circles all over my chest as if this is the first time they had ever explored the warmth of living human skin. As if this, too, will be the last time they linger on the skin of a being with a heartbeat. I keep on breathing. The smell of cigarette smoke and burned sandalwood mingles in my mind, and vividly, the Latin tattoo on his scarred wrist forges itself into existence. *Memento mori*.

"Hear that?" he whispers in the white stalk of hazy smoke.

His voice brings me back to the cruel nothingness of our reality. "What?" I ask, all absent-minded. My fingers dive into the thick brush of his curled-up hair, feeling the soft strands caress each tip.

"The beat. *Ba-dump. Ba-dump. Ba-dump.* Hey, what's your heart rate?"

"Normally, 70 bpm," I say, not knowing where this conversation is going, not even knowing why I am here or why we are still indulging in this horrible attempt at being normal while the catastrophe is avalanching toward us.

"Ain't it a little bit too fast for that rate?"

"'Cause this is not my normal," I say, catching his fingers within mine, which are dancing dangerously on my ribcage and my desire to swallow him whole and kiss each one of them. Slowly at first, then faster, I suck on them gently. I look into his eyes, imagining us burning in the forest fire atop our souls' mountain. "You're making it abnormal."

"How so?"

"Can I kiss you yet?"

"No. But have you ever thought about dying?" He withdraws his fingers from my firm grip and looks into my eyes.

I lose myself in his ocean of darkness, thinking, *What an inquisitive pair of eyes.* Too dark for the world. Too light for my desire. The moonlight outside the window shines its reflection on his dark irises. For a moment, I thought his eyes were the color of my mother's beautiful silver bracelet. I can see the dazzling jewels decorating the bracelet shift slowly from their position in the past to his black pupils that are boring holes into my heart every second as I breathe. *Damn,* I think to myself, *My sweet, golden, poisoned honey. You are killing me.*

"Have you ever thought about dying?" As I melt into the sweetness, that pair of eyes gently repeats that question like a broken record.

"I am. Thinking of it now. Can I at least touch your chest? Please, my darling? I can even settle for a little kiss."

"No, you must answer my question first," he chortles as his fingers form a weak barricade in front of his flat, bony chest. I can break the blockade easily with a twist of the fingers, but the rhythm of his heart makes me hesitate. Ba-dump. Ba-dump. Ba-dump. What's *his* heart rate?

"I already answered it," I retort, chasing away the dark thoughts, licking my lips, and feeling the heat burn my skin like a fiery torch.

"When?"

"I said I'm thinking of it now."

"Don't be a sulking child. Answer me."

"I really am thinking of it right here, right now. Quit it and just let me touch you." I inch closer. The down blanket and the mountain of pillows between us grow larger and heavier to get through. Who the fuck thinks of putting this many pillows on a bed? Not me.

"I'm also thinking about it." He exhales a white stalk of smoke, speaking in a soft monotone as if they are feathers. As if they mean he is free.

"Of what?"

"Dying."

I lift my head from the heavy blanket, but he turns away. Unconsciously, I keep begging him in my head. *Look at me, darling, look at me. Only at me.* But he is somewhere else. He is always somewhere else. Far beyond the oceans, the mountains, the moon, the sky. He is always one of the brightest stars, and I forever am the beggar standing beneath the heavens, begging, *Please, let the one you choose be me.*

"We're all dying, you know. Each and every one of us," he says. "I wonder what your response will be when I die. I'll lie here on the bed and say, 'Darling, I'm dying.' And you'll sit on that chair and say, 'Oh, don't die.' But will that ever stop me from dying?"

"What are you saying now? That won't stop anything."

"But you said it the other day."

"When?"

"I was lying here, sad and desolate. I said, 'Darling, I'm depressed.' Guess what you said then?" He smiles at me. A whole ocean breaks apart.

"I didn't mean it."

"Wrong. You said, 'Don't be depressed,'" he chuckles, puffing on the remains of his cigarette, and it breaks my heart into shards of glass, stabbing me in my lungs, punching me until there is nothing left to go on but the agony and the suffering pain of the living.

"I didn't mean it."

"Why? That cures me of my depression, darling. Don't you think that heals me of my depression?"

"I'm sorry."

"Why are you apologizing? I'm not punishing you. You know what, honey? Don't be sorry. Hey, let's have sex. Let's do it then, the thing you love most. Touch me."

And I touch him despite knowing that I'm a bastard and the worst human among all the living humans in this world; I still touch him. My palms hesitate on his chest. The veins on my fingers feel the warmth of his skin, the layer of bones on his ribcage, and the heart slowly beating behind it. I feel like crying. I don't even know why, but I suddenly feel like crying. This is one heartbeat. This is yet another heartbeat. And once my palm leaves this place, I can't feel it beating anymore. I firmly set my palms there and close my eyes. One, two, three—

"What are you doing?" he asks, catching my hands and

tugging at my fingers.

"I'm feeling it."

"What?"

"The living."

He cackles and detaches my octopus' fingers from his chest. "You're weird," he says as he throws the down blanket on the ground and swipes the mountain of pillows down the bed. It always amazes me how he can do the things I find impossible. "Listen, that's not what you should do."

He looks at me; his black irises promise an adventure of mischief and pleasure. His fingers slide down my chest but never really touch my skin. I quiver, tremulous, as he bends down; his breath touches the hollow between my neck and shoulder. His lips fall on my skin like spring rain. The dead skin is itchy, but the softness is still there. The scent of ripened peach and berries is so sickeningly sweet on his lips that I almost forget how to breathe and—

"What are you thinking, darling?"

"I'm not. Oh, God."

The kisses move lower and lower, with the same tempo as my current heartbeat. Just when I think he will finally kiss me in the right place, the kisses stop.

"What the hell?" I groan, feeling my patience drip away faster than the flow of time.

"I read a story the other day."

"The fuck are you doing?"

"Nothing. I just feel like this is the perfect time to tell this story."

He straddles me, tearing the condom open. As my desire grows exponentially with every labored breath he takes, he lowers his pulsing chest onto my chest and whispers his goddamned story. The hot breath on my skin feels like fire, and my skin keeps on burning, burning, burning for the glory of the living.

"And I like this quote about the story, you know," he says, lowering his hips. A soft hum escapes his lush lips.

"What quote?"

"Let's see. The sensei tells the student since he's a lonely man, he's glad that the student comes to visit him so often."

"And?" I try pushing my hips, but he holds me in place. His sheer willpower is enough to stop a war.

"Then he says since he is also a melancholy man, he can't help but doubt why the student wants to visit him so often."

"So?"

"I'm a melancholy man, darling," he smiles at me, "You don't see it so often, but my melancholy is always there. I sometimes wish there was a way for you to see it. Perhaps you can take it away from me."

As he says that, I feel like his breathing grows fainter. It's as if the warmth on my skin can disappear at any moment. As if I had been wrong right from the start. That I had picked the wrong side of the war; thus, I had grown to be person I detest. That he had chosen to follow the other route and the promise to see me on the other side of the war was all a lie because he did not pinky-swear on it. That we were children who grew up too quickly in a world that was not and never will be built for children. That his melancholy would be my melancholy someday, but the prophets did not tell me that yet.

"I want to see your melancholy," I say, my eyes growing heavy.

"You don't want to see it." He collapses onto my chest. From up close, his eyelashes fan out like a butterfly's wings. "You don't want to see it. You only say that so I can let you embrace me."

"You're wrong."

He ignores my words. "But I'll always let you embrace me." His fingers keep drawing these circles, and I don't know if I should be happy or sad. "That's how much I love you, darling. And that's how much I wish for you to love me."

"Why?"

"Because I'm a melancholy man."

He sits up. I can feel the heat from his core, and it keeps going lower, lower, lower. My hands catch onto the rough, round butt cheeks and squeeze them. He lets out a quiet sigh and then continues his journey. The soft flesh bounces back against my palms, and I can feel it tighten up, then relax, then tighten up, then relax. "It's good," I tell him.

"What's good?"

"This. This is good."

"Ha. Of course."

This is what I never tell you, I think while looking at him, bouncing up and down on top of my body. The downcast eyes, the tangled hair, the bony chest, the soft muscle on his stomach. All of it, all of it. *This is what I never tell you, my darling. This is what will haunt me. This is my biggest regret and my greatest comfort. This is what makes me chase after you, calling your name in the dark again and again.*

It's good, darling. It's good because you're alive.

"You're crying. Why are you crying?" He stops midway, leaning down to kiss away the tears I never knew I shed.

"Because you're beautiful."

"That so?"

"Yeah."

"But you don't call a man beautiful."

"That's sexist."

"That so? Stop crying. Come on, will 'don't be sad' work?"

"I can't live without you."

He stops his movement and looks at me. His eyes are like those of an orphan who has stayed in the orphanage for far too long, and when all humans have abandoned him, a family comes up and says, "Will you go home with us?"

"Don't lie," he says, "That's bad. Children shouldn't lie. We are grownups. Grownups don't need to rely on a single person to live happily."

"But that's the truth. Although there is no universal truth, and my truth will never be on the same level as yours. This is my declaration." I hold his face and make sure that he won't avert his eyes. "Look at me, darling. Look only at me because I can't live without you. I tried. I failed. My life without you has been nothing but hell."

"That's a lot of bullshit for someone who never thinks of dying."

He climbs down and returns to his pillow. His hand reaches for the lip balm on the nightstand, and he puts it on. The finger that just now was caressing my skin is on his lips, sliding back and forth, back and forth. He smacks his lips a few times, and the soft petals are now red when he finishes. Not the cold-or-blue-or-whatever-it-is red that the femme fatale wears on TV. It is a pinkish red with a sheen gloss. As he opens his mouth to sigh, the plump lips part with a soft sound as the sticky balm refuses to separate them.

"Can I kiss you?" I ask. The self-pity and the pathetic ring in my voice like a toll for the last desperate prayer of a fervent devout. Not to any god, but to almighty Love.

"What's with the sudden request?"

"No, but can I kiss you?"

"You do whatever the hell you want anyway."

"Of course."

He looks at me; his brows furrow impatiently. His gaze stops at my eyes for a little bit longer than normal—the kind of normal no one wants but must cope with anyway—and then he smiles. *You don't have to smile if you don't want to.* I want to tell him that, but I don't. And as years go by, I am less afraid of what I have done than what I didn't do.

"Can a kiss heal anything, though?" he says.

He reaches out to the windowpanes and opens them. Outside, the stars are fading away, just like whatever we have in this room, this very moment.

"You know, I heard a story." He gazes at the fading stars; his voice is as light as air.

"What story?"

"The stars we see right now are already dead."

"So?"

"Don't you think it's lonely? People only see them when they die shining. What about when they're suffering? What about when they're happy? Or when they have an exciting story, but the only living being there is rocks and dirt?"

"But we appreciate their beauty, though, right? Like right now, we can see that they're stunning."

I sit up, push him over, and lie down on his stomach. Somehow, my body is all heavy, and I just want to sleep forever on his warm belly. Amidst the drowsiness and the border of dreams, I hear him talking to me, ever so soft and gentle. "My darling, darling, darling..."

Honey, it's not about us. It's all about them.

Honey, feel it? This is warmth. This is a heartbeat. This is living.

Honey, have you ever realized what a marvelous coincidence it is when we are the only living things in this vast universe of dying stars?

Honey, humans are beautiful.

But honey, oh, honey, humans are incredibly lonely.

And honey, if God indeed does love us as they say in the Bible, how can He make humans such lonesome creatures?

Honey, honey, honey—

Honey, what if I die tomorrow?

* * *

I hear a loud bell ringing constantly, one after another. My head is all heavy, and my mind is hazy. It's as if I'm dreaming about a world that would never be. I turn off the alarm on my phone. Then, the one on my nightstand. Then, the one on the work station across the bed. Then, the one on the window's edge. All the places that he used to touch, live, and breathe., and breathe.

It's been one year since the day he tried to fly. But the earth's gravity was too strong, and instead of being an angel beside God, he was just a mess—a mixture of blood, bones, flesh, and my will to go on living after witnessing his death.

I look into the dressing mirror. Who's there? Is it me? Or is it him? It seems the monster who took him away from me has finally decided to possess me. But never mind, never mind.

The phone rings. A familiar name appears, but it triggers no fond memory.

"Hey, wanna get lunch today? I tried calling in the morning, but I failed," our mutual friend calls out from the speaker. His voice is too loud for my ears right after waking up. The nightmare of moving on repeats itself once more.

I stare at my reflection in the mirror, and the monster in me asks him over the phone: "Hey, have you ever thought about dying?"

Another Day in the Life

He sits there, under the burning sun of a country that has long ago forgotten him. Counting the people hurrying by in the blazing heat of this unforgiving weather, he thinks, *Man, I would kill to have a nice cup of iced tea.* And indeed, free iced tea is available everywhere on the street. But whenever he reaches out for that free iced tea, infused with a dose of pity and a shot of unhidden contempt, he feels like he shrinks a little in size. As if that iced tea is a magical potion that has the ability to metamorphose him into a kind of insect, the insects that live on this street, feed on the trash, and overall, make the city less beautiful in the eyes of the foreign beings with blonde hair and blue eyes. The sky clouds over, as if heaven is looking out for her unfortunate children in a rare moment of benevolence, and the harsh reality of his life comes back to him.

What if he cannot sell all the lottery tickets? Is it true that picking up trash and recyclable stuff is a better job than what he has in hands right now? The sweat drops fall into his eyes; the spicy, parched taste burns his tongue, and across the street, there's another lottery ticket seller.

"Man, I would kill to have a nice cup of iced tea," he grumbles and stands up. His left knee is killing him softly, gradually, easing him to a nice and slow death. The right knee, well, let's say the right stump, because there is no leg left there, is doing fine. He takes that as a win. One has so very little chance of winning in this life. Take whatever you can get; that is his motto.

He waves the lottery tickets in front of the people riding by the busy intersection without an energetic wave to show the people that he cares enough. Neither is it an inviting wave to show that he wants to sell the tickets. He has long forgotten for what purpose he waves them; someone might stop; someone might care enough to buy. And yes, that's the kind of wave he's showing the world: a wave that ignites the pity in the passersby, a wave with death's shadow cast in his eyes, a wave to show that, like those passersby, he's tired of the living, that he's only doing this because he can't choose death and he can't choose how his life turns out at the end of the day. He has no wife. He has no kids. He just has poverty perched on his shoulders. He never wishes for it to be there, but since his wife and kids died in that bombing raid, the poverty decided to choose him as one of its many victims. He often thinks of it as winning the lottery, except that instead of money, he has won a lifetime of skimming through trash cans and sleeping on the pavement.

"Man, would I kill to have a nice cup of iced tea," he says to himself, and walks across the street.

He never cares much for the oncoming traffic. Whether he dies today or another day, it doesn't matter. He would just add to the statistics of death by traffic incidents and, give it another day or two, he would be forgotten. He thinks about how people can easily forget the many lives who lost their chance of winning on the street and yet, no matter how hard he tries, he cannot forget about his wife and sons.

He replays the scene of the bombing raid. It moves in frames like an old black-and-white film roll. He was shooting the enemies—and by enemies, he means whoever came up to him, because why should death discriminate?—and just as the war was won, the enemies gone, the planes stored up in museums, he came home to the scattered pieces of his wife and infant sons. The house was torn down. He didn't even gather enough of the pieces to cremate his wife, not to mention his sons.

He just stood there amidst the chaos, and he felt a sense of calm. The calm that made him wonder, why did he fight? For the motherland? For his people? Or for his wife and infant sons? Why was he allowed to kill at the age of 15? The age where he first learned to love another human was the age he learned to pick up a gun and shoot another human at point-blank range. And the corpses there on the fields, were they enemies or were they his comrades? He could not have known; they shared the same skin color, the same short and sturdy stature, the same blood, the same bone. If he were given enough time to learn about them before killing them, he would have probably known that their mothers and his shared some sort of connection.

Don't think, comrade, don't think, just shoot, for fuck's sake, just shoot.

Those were his comrade's last words before he was blown to pieces in the bombing raid, along with many others, of course. But to him, when he stood in front of the torn house and the scattered flesh, those deaths meant so little. People die in war; so what? Should he care more because they are closer to his heart? Should he also care for the strangers and the enemies? His heart was not that big, and he believed no human's heart ever was. He looked at the sky turning dark with little spots of stars, wondering if there was a God. He was a communist. He should not be wondering about deities.

But in front of that ending scene of his blown-up house and his blown-up wife, he just wondered if it's true what they said, that as long as you lived a good life, as long as you were a decent human, the gods would protect you. He lit up a cigarette, inhaled, and as he exhaled the white, whirling smoke, he thought, *Man, would I kill to have a nice cup of iced tea.*

And he cried. The only time that he would cry. Throughout the war, there was a silent ban on grieving. He couldn't mourn the death of his comrades. Abandoning the corpses was a normal practice. He questioned his superior many times, "Who will bring them home?" And they answered, "History." Fuck that. No history will stand witness to the loss of innocence. He bet his youth on something as fragile as an ideology. Will it resurrect his people? Yes, he calls them all people, enemies or comrades. They are all Vietnamese. The more he thought about that fucking war, the more tears came out. Big, nasty tears that tasted like the blood of his motherland. She didn't choose this war; he knew that most of all. It came upon her like a savage who never learned the sincerity in the word "sorry." History will bring them home; he cursed at the saying loud and clear. But history is written by the victor, and in the flourishes of those letters, he wouldn't find the fear and trembling of his young friends, who, besides the indoctrinated hatred and vengeance, also had in them the seed of dreams.

As the people cheered for victory, he cheered for death. He took the medals, the decorations, the stars and whatnot, and returned to what his life had been before the war. Same old poverty. Same old life of skimming through trash cans and sleeping on pavement. The only difference was that he was older, lost a leg, wounded an arm. What was left of him was a remnant of what was defined as a human being.

Don't think, comrade, don't think. Just shoot.

Shoot at what? he thinks as he continues along the pavement. His crutches drag along as the sky darkens in anticipation of rain. Forgive me, comrade, for I tried not to think, but when death keeps staring you in the face, it's hard for you not to think. He was taught to kill, but he was not taught how to live on after his killings. He was taught not to think, but he was not taught how to stop thinking. He was taught a lot in the war, but he was not taught how to keep on living after it. The war outlived everyone, and when he stepped into it, he never thought that he would be among the living.

He stops at another intersection and waves the tickets. No one stops to buy them. People renounced luck long ago. They believe more in the deities' goodwill, but they don't have enough faith to hold up their end of the bargain: living decently. He thinks about his life after the bombing. Did he live decently enough? After all these years, was he able to compensate for all he killed? The wind blows some of his tickets away and he walks slowly into the oncoming traffic to pick them up amid the shouting and yelling of the people. No one notices his soldier uniform. No one notices his medals, his decorations, his stars and whatnot. He also stopped noticing them long ago. He crosses the intersection, takes a left turn, and walks into the alley. He rummages through his shirt pocket. A ten thousand note and a five thousand note. He spent the rest of it on flowers for his wife and infant sons. Today marks their death anniversary, and as any decent husband would, he prepares dishes and flowers for their frugal graves. He thinks of it as a ritual to prove to himself that he is still living, that he still has a part of humanity within him, broken and shattered, but human, nonetheless.

He stands under the tin roof of a house. Next to him, an old lady is selling pancakes. Another old lady is crouching down to pick up recycling. He is not sure what is on her back. It seems that, unlike him, she has carried on her crouched back something heavier than poverty. Something like other humans' lives. He wonders, had his wife been still alive, would she be crouching, too? He remembers, when he had not been there, his wife had a life he'd never known. All he could see from the remnant of the torn-up house was the empty baby crib, the shattered rainwater jars, and his parents' altar. He has spent half of his life trying to figure out why God only allowed those things to survive. And for the other half, he has tried to imagine what life had would been like with only those things as his lonesome companions. Here is his wife, carrying his infant sons, one on her back and another on her side. Here, she uses the rainwater to cook the rice and water the garden. Here is his wife again, taking care of his parents' altar the same way she'd taken care of them when they were alive. She'd pour them water, light incense, change the fruit dish every two days. Not that expensive fruit dish that people put on the altar nowadays; just a very simple fruit dish from the back garden. Sometimes, there'd be an additional meat dish, if she could bargain with the seller. With all of the work she had put into living, he has no doubt that she would be crouching like that old lady if she were still alive.

Across the street, people are bustling about. He stands and watches life passing through him ever so gently, ever so briefly, like the spring wind. He never stops marveling at how this life can move on at whatever pace it wants, leaving behind a trace of suffering, pain, and death. As if it never cares for those whose fate intertwines with it, and the more you love life, the more it will leave you hanging. But once in a while, when life is bored with itself and decides to turn around to show you some affection—a kiss, a touch, a smile—you suddenly come to a stop with all that hatred and vengeance. For the first time ever, you see life for what it is: its beauty, its gentleness, its pulsing heart in the palm of your hands. *And at such times*, he thinks, *all that suffering and pain are not that hard to bear.* He will try to find his way around it. If he can't face it directly, he will walk around it. And when he gathers enough courage, he will let life take him on that journey. Perhaps on that journey, he will see his wife again, forever at the age of twenty, and he goes back to being the boy of twenty-three, where he will have just enough happiness to forget about the war, the lottery tickets, the medals, the decorations, the stars and whatnot.

The rain washes over the city. The pancake seller hurriedly gathers her stove and utensils. People stop along the alley to put on their raincoats. *Well,* he thinks, *there it goes. Another day in my life.* He wouldn't be able to sell the rest of his tickets. He would owe the ticket distributor another hefty sum of money that both she and he knew he wouldn't be able to pay back. He would find somewhere to sleep for the night, somewhere with good cover—a tin roof, perhaps—so that he could listen to the rain washing his life away. His heaviest worries right now are his crutches and his bag, where he stores his parents' and his wife's photos. His life lies within them; and they are the line on which he hangs his hopes and dreams to dry. He wonders, sometimes, whatever happens to living happily ever after once all the wars have ended? And what about the future of disabled veterans like him, who betted their lives against the bloodshed and gunshots so the smile could grace the children's faces? He never thought one day, the things he sacrificed will be reduced to dust, and people will go on killing one another, filled with hatred and division. This is not the peace he had fought with blood and tears for. But nothing matters now. He walks out into the rain to the newly appeared trash bag and rummages through it. He scores a half-empty milk carton, and he drinks it all up. His tattered, threadbare shirt is all wet. The lines on his face are accentuated by the rainwater. He looks like a crumpled-up piece of paper, only darker, poorer, and no one would think of straightening him out to reuse him, to read through his life, to write down on it something as bitter as love, as sweet as suffering.

"Man, would I kill to have a nice cup of iced tea," he says.

He sits down under the tin roof, in front of the metal door frame of a brick house, and takes out his patched blankets. The sky is darkening. The night casts a long, unfathomable shadow over the brightly lit city like the eyelashes of a maiden fanning over her youthful, poignant face. The cold breeze leaves cuts and scratches on his amputated leg and his shrapnel-filled arm. He curls up into a fetal position and thinks about his mother. She was a brave woman, braver than anyone he has ever met during his weary lifetime. She often prayed in front of the altar; she had wanted nothing more than a fulfilling life for her many children. Perhaps the ancestors did not hear her prayers. Perhaps God had deemed her prayers so damn unworthy. None of her children—save for him—survived. She kept praying, nonetheless. Her faith was beyond the shadow of death, beyond the hopes and dreams, and even beyond life itself.

He lies down on the hard porch, pulls his blankets over his

head, and immerses himself in the warm pool of imagination. He sees his mother standing there, in front of the altar. Her back is also crouched, her gray hair pulled up into a tiny bun behind her head, her thin neck filled with wrinkles. She wears her usual black blouse and pants, with so many patches that one could not know if her clothes were indeed black to start with. Her most valuable treasure was the pearl earrings that she always had on her earlobes. She said she would leave them to her eldest daughter, his sister, on the day she got married. The promise was never fulfilled. And as he sees her there, praying, with her eyes closed and her lips moving briefly, murmuring the prayers, he thinks about his future. What can he do from here on out? He has outlived many people in his family. He has outlived life itself, as his mother had wished, and now, he wonders if he can outlive death. His head grows heavy, and he slowly falls into sleep's embrace.

One of these mornings, people will find him lying in front of their house, or in front of a stone wall, cold and hard. They will see his medals, his decorations, his stars and whatnot. They will know that he sacrificed his youth, his family, and a part of his life for the motherland. They will weep. They will talk about how they should have recognized him and treated him better. But none of that will matter to him; he has lived for the motherland and now, he will return to the close embrace of the motherland. And if the motherland ever asks him what his wish had been when he was alive, he will just give her a feeble smile and say, "Man, would I kill to have a nice cup of iced tea."

Until the Darkness Beyond

*O*ne night, walking back home on the small valley
I chance upon the late-blooming baby rose
Perhaps the delicate hand that once touched those petals
Is now no longer remembering the old garden—

The song keeps mournfully reverberating off the whitewashed walls like a broken record echoing from the depth of a dusty, bygone past. If he squeezed his eyes tight enough, he could almost taste the lukewarm, sickening sweetness of guilt and shattered conscience on the tip of his tongue. The pills the nurse gave him this morning now slowly dissolve in his mouth. He never swallows them straightaway. He only gives the impression that he does so. The nurse never lets any suspicion show on her face. The nurse silently knows. He loves this feeling—letting the bitterness of the pills remind him that some parts of his body are still reacting to life. That he is still living. Breathing through his nose. Filling his lungs with the scent of sunlight filtering through the barred windows and the stale, damp smell of the locked room.

Chewing on the pills, he thinks about the plan. The escape route. How many times will this make? He doesn't care. He has given up on counting. The only thing he can register through the tedious days is the way the sun rises on the horizon each morning. And the night. The long, arduous night. He doesn't sleep anymore. He fears the monsters creeping along the walls and the winding corridors that will jump out and bite his throat whenever he closes his eyes. He is not afraid of death. He never was. What crawls on his skin, gnaws at his flesh, gouges his heart, is the prospect that somewhere in that nightmare, the monsters will force him to see. To look in the mirror. To confront the worst beast known to mankind: himself.

Tick tock. Tick tock. Tick tock. He counts the seconds until the doctor's visit. Dangling his feet, he imagines the shuffling of the white smock outside, the twisting of the doorknob, the clattering of folders and the screeching of chairs on the floor. He sits up, facing the normal routine. The facade. The masquerade. The theatrical stage he is unwillingly a part in, no matter how small.

"How are you doing?" the doctor asks, flipping through the files.

"Fine. Grand. Never been better. Multiple choice answer. Pick whatever fits your career advancement."

"Let me put it this way. You've been refusing treatment, and it falls under my care to investigate—"

"Yeah, keep on talking. I don't mind listening to your professional terminology for one hour."

"Mr. Nguyen."

"There's no Mr. Nguyen. He died long ago. What you see is a construction of society's imagination of what Mr. Nguyen should be like if he were still living. Mr. Nguyen should never be living."

"In a way, you mean you are traumatized by the event of—"

"In a way, I mean that you're wasting your time. No one tries to resurrect a ghost."

"But it causes no harm."

"Everyone thinks that. Until they try. Until it does."

"I mean it causes no harm to love the living." The doctor sighs; he knows it is going to be a long session, an eternity compressed into the limited span of one hour.

"Do I look like I don't love the living?"

"If you love them, would you still be here?"

"I don't know. One can love the living and still be crazy. And vice versa. One can be sane and hate it to the bone."

"Hate what?"

"The living."

"Which side are you on, then?"

"Whichever is the last one standing."

"So you don't want to die, at least?"

"I don't want to lose."

"Usually, not wanting to lose is the first sign of a willingness to live."

"In which universe?"

"In all of them, I would think."

"Have you been to every universe, then?"

"I have not."

"Then leave a little bit for the imagination."

"And in your imagination, will there be a universe where there's no willingness to live?"

"No, in my imagination, this universe is the only one where there's no willingness to live. Yet people persist. Stubbornly. Obstinately. Like a sore loser on a betting table who never learns the meaning of defeat."

"And to you, is that a good thing or a bad thing?"

"If I knew, I would be out there fighting."

"You mean you surrendered?"

"I mean I'd tried. Hard. And I'd failed. Many times. Far too many. I refuse to stand up one more time. That's what I did."

"Mr. Nguyen, have you ever thought about how things would change if one specific event, for lack of a better word, was different?"

"And was it different?"

"I said if…"

"So you want me to play make-believe with the kind of degree you possess."

"We have to put things in perspective."

"My perspective is clear. There's only one way. The way we are on."

"I heard from the nurse that you haven't been able to sleep."

"Haven't been. Hadn't been. Never. Pick whatever fits your code book."

"I don't need a code book for insomnia."

"You will need a code book for the degree of craziness you want to categorize me in."

"You have a very skeptical outlook on psychiatrists and mental illness."

"I have no outlook. On anything. I float. Sometimes I'm anchored to this bed. Sometimes I'll be up there. The monsters are everywhere, and I need a place to hide."

"You mention the monsters every time we meet."

"And yet you fail to save me from them. To that I say, a job well done."

"Mr. Nguyen."

"Time's up."

He watches the doctor leave through the slits of his half-closed eyes. The exhaustion drags him down, down, down like the soft cradle of a mother. The song halts, then resumes its torturous melody. *Love, it's my dream, a beautiful dream.* He has a sense that he is drowning. The water is closing in. He is suffocating with his own breath. If only this would be the end of it. Life as he knows it on earth fades away into darkness. He chews on the pills, but they are no longer there. He stares at the clock on the wall, waiting for the sun to set.

Nine-thirty p.m. He watches the face of the digital clock glower in red. The darkness descends like a thick, velvety curtain draws over the stage. The people are gone. He waits for someone to come and clean up the props: the blanket, the pillowcase, the drape, and the imaginary dead goldfish he sees on the nightstand. They can leave the imaginary dead goldfish. No matter how many times they try to pick it up, the fish keeps slipping through their fingers and remains where it is. Its eyes bore bleeding holes into his face. He doesn't hate it, but sometimes, when the weather changes, and the wind howls outside in a belligerent cry, the imaginary goldfish reminds him how much he wants to call it quits on this thing called life. The cart rolls past his room; the clattering of metal against invisible, stifling, ether scent rings in his ears until the silence crawls back into his bed and snuggles close to his side.

"It is coming," the silence says.

"What is coming?" he asks.

"The monster," the silence replies.

"The monster," he repeats.

On the wall, he witnesses with his own eyes as the plaster peels off in chunks, revealing the red, angry layering of bricks beneath it. The fleeting shadow slides down, pooling around his feet. A hand grasps his ankle. The fingers are stripped of skin. What remains is just a perfect combination of flesh and broken bones. The slimy digits climb up his legs, dragging him off the bed, and he lets them. He closes his eyes, thinking, *Here we go again.* The silence says, "Yes, yes, yes." He sinks to the nightmare, embracing it like a long-lost friend. On nights like these, he gets lonely and desperate enough to forgive life, its misery, and what he has done to himself. And other nights, he will let the monster win. He will always let the monster win.

One day, walking back from the bustling marketplace
  Suddenly a gladness overwhelms me like a child
  Perhaps my life has forever been a fire
  Waiting to burn in a night garden—

He opens his eyes; the sun is already rising. Torture is the night, but he always longs for it when it is gone. He yearns for the pain. It is the only sign for him to know that he is still breathing. He tries to lift his arms, but halfway through the process, he gives up. As with everything else in his life at this point, he gives up. Lying there, he thinks about the doctor and the conversation they had yesterday. The same conversation that they will have today, tomorrow, and many tomorrows after that. He wonders what great force is behind the doctor's living, what keeps him awake at night. And most importantly, what urges him to wake up, day after day, month after month, year after year. The doctor seems like he has seen better days. Then again, he thinks, everyone has always seen better days. The question is, will there be better days ahead? He drifts away in the slanted sunlight. People think he will miss the air outside. The seasons in the sun. But he stops caring about that. No matter what fancy terms they put on it, or the pretty labels and decorations they string around their houses, to him, time is just time. It flows and it flows and it flows. People say, "Enjoy the journey." He says, "I'd rather see the end." The doorknob twists. He glances over. The doctor stands there in his majestically white smock. "I hope you had a good night's rest," the doctor says.

"As good as it gets. Can't complain. Can't wish for more. Pick whatever phrase fits your playbook."

"So now you call my diagnosis a playbook."

"Everything is a playbook. You just have to abide by the rules."

"And are you someone who'll abide by the rules?"

"You choose. I end up here."

"Let's talk about something else. Something less complicated."

"Like what?"

"In your file, the previous psychiatrists put that you're a brave soldier. But they also say that you're a difficult patient."

"There's no correlation or causation, whichever perspective you choose to take."

"I mean, how is life on the battlefield?"

"Normal. You try to survive until you don't."

"You fought for your country, didn't you?"

"I fought for what I believed in. Until I didn't. Until the war stopped."

"Mr. Nguyen, is it safe to say that you hold an idealistic, bordering on extreme nationalistic, love for your country?"

"It's safe to say that I love my country. It's never safe to say whether it is a nationalistic love or an idealistic one. I don't. Anymore."

"Does one just stop loving one's own country?"

"One will love one's own country until one realizes that no matter how much love one pours into it, the country can't love him back."

"Your country doesn't love you back."

"My country tried."

"Did it succeed?"

"It's still trying."

"But you've given up."

"It changes. I think it'll be the same beautiful existence after the bloodshed. But it suffers enough bloodshed that instead of succumbing to the hands of the executors, it turns itself into a murderess. It wields in its hands an axe and a scythe. It uses false ideals and cruel indoctrination to kill the people who had tried so hard to protect the innocence of what is still left underneath the earth. I know my country is hurt. I know the wounds are still bleeding. And though my country is still trying, the loving is hard to see. The loving is never there. Anymore."

"You see your country as a person."

"I defend it as one. Why can't I think of it as one?"

"Let's change the subject."

"Why? I like the current subject."

"Talking about wars will get us nowhere."

"I disagree. If anything, talking about wars is the only way we move forward. In fact, wars are the one thing people ever talk about. From the birth of the first human to the death of the last, there will always be wars."

"Do you like wars, then?"

"I fought them. What do you think?"

"One can fight a war and hate it. Vice versa; one can fight a war and like it."

"Or one can fight a war and do just that, fight a war."

"Did you lose anyone you love in the war?"

"Let's change the subject."

"Grief, then. Let's talk about how we deal with grief."

"That's interesting."

"The subject?"

"No. The idea that you think I have grief."

"People have grievances. Losing someone dear to them. Going through traumatizing events. Having to bear a burden more than they can tolerate. There are many ways a person can break."

"I don't."

"You don't break?"

"Grieve. I don't grieve. I'd been broken long ago. Forsaken for a higher indifference."

"You talk like you still want to be saved, Mr. Nguyen, and I'm here for that. We're all here for that."

"I talk like I want to end it. And you're not here for that. No one wants an ending. They want things to last."

"Let's talk about your best friend."

"The one who died."

"The one who died in your arms."

"Heh. Of course, because you always want what hurts the most. Fits the description of the mental illness in your category book, doesn't it? And it's easier for you to prescribe another pill."

"Why don't we agree that I'm trying to help?"

"Because no one helped when we were out there fighting to survive."

"And how did that make you feel?"

"Give me the pill first. Write this down so you have enough

proof for your avant-garde diagnosis later. The boy who died in my arms, he was so young. About twenty years old. These days, I often imagine hearing his voice. Under the deepest blue sky, he shouted out. My name on his lips sounded like a person's. He stood before me, his rifle slung heavily on his back with a thousand little things in his backpack. Among them, you can find a diary. He wrote diligently. I never knew what he intended to do with all those rigorous writings. They didn't save him in the end. Nothing ever did. I remembered flipping through the pages. The ink on them hadn't had the chance to dry yet before he breathed his last. In the neat pen of a college graduate, he mulled, 'Why are we fighting? And why are we killing the other side? Aren't we all human?' And they killed him. They shot him down. The only human who ever lived in a war."

"You are haunted by his death."

"I am not. Never. Haunted."

"But he has a special existence in your memory."

"Not anymore."

"Is it safe to say that he has now remained as the monster that you talk about in your sessions?"

"I won't begrudge him for that."

"Mr. Nguyen, that's grief. And that's your way of dealing with grief."

"Time's up."

He closes his eyes and lets his memory roam free. He wanders across the ocean and walks along the fields. His hands dig into the undulating, ripening rice stalks. The yellow rice grains feel heavy in his palms. The water is up to his knees. The mud drags his heels gently back with every step forward. He looks up from his camouflage. The leaves are covering his eyes as the

August sunlight slants through the bamboo groves. Standing there, taller than the piling regrets he would have, a giant soul in the frame of a young boy, is his best friend. He screams, "Watch out." He'd screamed that phrase a million times in his mind, and he would scream it still until the end of time. But the film keeps rolling. He is just another observer, watching the repetition of the same old pain as his heart is gouged out, again and again. The boy takes a step forward in the dike, and then, he fell down, into that darkness, deeper, deeper, everything he ever was finally reduced to the fading glimpse of a beaming smile in the summer heat as the writing ran in the background like a loudspeaker in a noir film: "Why are we fighting? Aren't we all human?"

He hears footsteps in the hallway. Someone is approaching. He can feel their presence creeping in the encroaching darkness. The noise is closing in. He wonders if he should put on the record and keep it playing until morning. He thinks he hears people talking. Their conversation is muddled because their sentences overlap with one another. One never ends and one never fully begins. He tries to find in that chaotic storm of words and static signals a way to leave. The labyrinth of the memory traps him from all sides, and he keeps running, but he doesn't know which way is the exit. He feels the air shift, but when he turns that way, the door closes again.

"Be silent," he murmurs, "Be silent. I almost found my escape route. I'm almost free."

The doctor says, "That is grief, and that is how you deal with grief, Mr. Nguyen."

Tick tock. Tick tock. Tick tock. The clock moves in the dark. The red glow of the digits burns his retinas as he stares at the slow changing of time. The doorknob twists, or he imagines it does. As he turns toward the source of the noise, he sees the young boy standing there, leaning on the rifle. His camouflage is stained a deep burgundy, and his smile is just a gaping, black hole. "Hello," he says. "Never knew you could get here. Usually they lock the insane outside."

"I know," the young boy says, or he thinks the boy does, because it is hard to see from the shadow cast on his face.

"It's been a long time."

"I know."

"Are you here to pick me up?"

The boy doesn't reply, or he thinks the boy stays silent. It is just a figment of his imagination. He doesn't care if the boy answers or not. But sometimes, it gets so lonely that he wishes he could hear the ghosts talk. He pricks his ears. Far down the hall, he can detect the sound of exploding bombs. "That is grief, Mr. Nguyen," the doctor says. And he never believes it. The pretty labels, the fancy names, the detailed definitions to categorize humans into different levels of invisible pain and leave them there, trapped to death. He'd rather choose another ending. But here he is, still living on the meager mercy of the government he defends. The thanks he gets for being the last one standing. He is starving for a cheap cigarette. The hunger is such a sudden rush that he can feel its claws scratching inside his stomach. The moon slants through the slats on the windows, and he lets himself be distracted for a while.

Nine forty-five p.m. The footsteps are getting nearer and nearer. The marching of soldiers to battlefields, never to return. The promises of victory, guaranteed at a steeper cost than anyone could have bargained for. The oath to be together, no matter what, to survive, no matter what, to get back in one piece, no matter what.

"But it does matter, doesn't it?" he asks.

The boy stares at him through two black holes where his eyes are supposed to be. A silence that borders on strangling breath forces him to look back.

"You know, I'd watched you every day," he pleads to the disfigured, limping ghost of the boy. The tears shine in his eyes with a newfound madness of bliss and blessing.

"I know."

"Something in me always told me that it wouldn't end well. You or me. Neither will end well."

"I know."

"And I still persist."

"I know."

"I used to fear death, and now I fear life." He reaches for the boy's embrace. Nothing is there for him but the cold, stale air of the isolation room.

"I know."

"How's life over there?"

The boy stays silent, as if his only purpose in being there in the room is to let the man know that he exists. Conscience exists. The guilt of being alive exists. The marching keeps on through the night. He never closes his eyes. The moonlight washes over his face in gentle waves of soft, silvery wind. He didn't know he had it in him, but he starts longing for the return of the psychiatrist. By the first ray of morning light, the boy vanishes. The hunger stays. And he dies slowly as the day bleeds into another, merging into a giant block of wasted time.

In the night garden, a secret flower is just blooming
 Has someone just passed by my weary life?

Sometimes I can't help but think
The hundreds of graves are still here, crying
Our life seems to have no other new desire
And I have been living on fever dreams—

The psychiatrist listens through the closed door. The same song has been on repeat for days. Or months. Or years. For as long as the man's been here.

"How is he doing?" the doctor asks.

"Normal," the nurse replies, checking the vital signs on her clipboard.

"Really?"

"Yes, doctor."

"Then why does he keep on staring at the clock so gravely? And that song. He seems to have a strange obsession with it."

"I'm not sure, sir."

"I wonder where he will end up. I have togo home now, but you should spend more time with him. He seems distraught, especially around this time in April."

"Sir, with all due respect, I don't think anyone who enters this place ever leaves."

"Our aim, or rather, my aim, is to have him leave, well-adjusted to society and happy."

"Sir." The nurse stares at the doctor with weary and tired eyes. "Do you think that being outside is what he desires? After all these years?"

"It doesn't matter what I think. It's the high benefit of society."

"He doesn't have a family."

"Here's hardly a good place to stay."

"But it'll be a good place to end."

"I think he'll do better if he has a little love and care in his life."

"And he doesn't think so, sir."

"It's the system. I'm grateful for how it leads us forward, but sometimes, the system breaks people."

"The system has been breaking people since forever."

"I'm going home."

The psychiatrist walks away with leaden footsteps. The nurse rolls her cart into the dark hallway. The corridor is heavy with the breathing of the insane and the sane, confined to the same place, locked in the same maze. The man inside the locked room stops the song for a minute, listening to the sound of the night, then he resumes playing the song again. Eyes closed, he's drowning, waiting for the ghosts to return.

Tick tock. Tick tock. Tick tock.

Ten a.m. He stares at the psychiatrist sitting opposite him.

"It stopped," he says.

"What did?"

"The footsteps. The marching soldiers. The sound of people discussing what they would do on the day they return home. They were talking still."

"Mr. Nguyen, let's talk about your auditory hallucinations. Will you say they're getting worse?"

"Call it what you want. Hallucination. Imagination. Shadows of the bygone past. Your choice."

"And your choice is?"

"It's real. As real as life can get for me."

"What are the soldiers talking about?"

"The day they return."

"What will they do?"

"Get married. Continue their studying. Have a meal with their mothers. Their wives are waiting. Their newborn children are learning their first words. Life will go on. One way or another, life will go on."

"And then?"

"Nothing." The man watches the sunlight dancing on the barred windows. "None of them return. Only me. There was only ever me."

"Mr. Nguyen, if one hears sounds that no one else can, that is categorically an auditory hallucination."

"Does your fancy term make my life less real?"

"Mr. Nguyen, the point of hallucination is that it's never real. And we can treat that."

"Hush. Doctor, do you hear that?"

"Hm? What?"

"It's the sound. So loud that it's drowning out your voice."

"What sound?"

"The sound of liars trying to prove that there's a point in killing one another and watching the corpses burn to build a world that will never be."

"Mr. Nguyen, I think—"

"I don't. Think. Time's up."

The psychiatrist walks briskly out the door. The song plays insistently in the background like a funeral eulogy.

Some nights I dream of being a waterfall
  Waking up, I can still hear the echoes—

The room becomes darker and darker still as the clock on the wall shows the first sign of midnight. He shrivels up inside the corner, shivering, his teeth clattering. His eyes scan the room for the young boy. The ghost refuses to come. He watches in fear and trembling as the thick canopies of the deadly forest are resurrected in front of him. People are screaming. Feet are trampling upon bodies. *Breathe*, he reminds himself. *It's nothing you haven't seen before.* But something was wrong. Is it just him or is the clock smiling? Tick tock. Tick tock. Tick tock. The marching reverberates in the hallway, outside the walls, in the open fields, far down the playground. *It's coming*, he thinks. *They're coming. To get me.* He looks at the door. The boy is there, from time unknown.

"I heard your voice," he says, his words growing tremulous and tender. "You called out my name."

"I know."

"I thought you would never accept it, so I kept it buried inside my heart. I let it smolder until the embers burnt the tips of my fingers when they touched your melting skin. Your corpse was slipping through the cracks of my hands. I held onto the flesh like the last salvation. You never returned."

"I know."

"How much more do I have to pay? The price is getting higher than what I can afford. And I no longer have it in me to live another day."

"I know."

"I don't even remember it anymore. The way your eyes twinkled in the moonlit nights on the battlefields. The way you smiled like you were the happiest fool when you showed me your poems. Your voice when you whispered my name, telling me a joke only us two would understand. Your laugh. Show me—show me, please, where the suffering begins."

"I know."

"I let it burn. The love was never lost. But you're no longer here. And I can't cross over there. Tell me. Are you still waiting? And is it fun, torturing me with this immense yearning? I'm bleeding every day, prostrating myself in front of the altar of what could have been, consoling myself with the thought that one day, we'll see each other again."

"I know."

"And maybe, maybe after all these wars, after all the lives are shed, I will have enough courage to tell you how much I had—"

The footsteps are getting nearer. He cranes his neck to listen to the pain singing. The marching stops in front of his room, then passes right through it. He looks at the clock, waiting, expecting, longing. As the red digits glow their way to midnight, he rocks himself back and forth, thinking of a million ways to uninstall himself from the earth. To never exist. To never be. Softly, he mumbles the song.

I have closed my heart, far too many times
  Only to kneel by my bleeding wounds
  Because you have taken my sincerest prayers
  And left me in this quiet solitude on life's roadside—

A loud clattering sound breaks his trance. He looks to the record player in the left corner of the whitewashed room. The old disc is broken into a thousand tiny pieces. *Of course*, he thinks. How can one little record endure the passage of slow, cruel time? It has run on for as long as it can. Since the day he was admitted to the psychiatric ward, he has made a silent oath that the day the record breaks will be the day his life ends. He takes one last look around. The room is deathly silent now. The curtain is slowly drawing closed, with emptiness enveloping the cramped space. He takes a bow. The role is done. Whether it is performed splendidly or not, he has no right to judge. He guesses from the lack of applause that he hasn't done that well, but he won't ask for forgiveness, and he'd rather end on this bad note than play it all over again. The boy finally approaches him in small steps. He tries to find love where there's only ever been wounds.

"I love you," he says.

"I know," the boy says, kneeling. One of his eyes sparkles to life.

"I've always loved you. Since the first day of killing and the last day of surrendering. I've always survived on the thought of you."

"Yes, I know."

"You promised that you would return."

"And I didn't." The boy smiles. Thin, pale lips appear where a black hole usually is.

"I promised that I would forget."

"And you didn't."

"How much pain was in your wallet the day you were blown up by that bomb?"

"As much as life can offer. As much as I can get."

"You always had a hunger for suffering."

"And you always tolerated the hurt."

"I knew that you would come to get me."

"And I did."

"You know that I will wait for you, patiently."

"And you did."

"People think I'm crazy."

"Only the craziest people are the happiest."

"Where are our comrades?"

"They're outside."

"And you'll take me to them."

"Better. I'll take you where peace resides."

101

"No love lost."

"No blood found."

The clock strikes midnight. The man climbs out the window, slithers through the bars. His figure has grown thin enough to escape the prison of the insane. He stands on the balustrade, his lips trembling. The marching band is below, playing in the garden. His comrades are urging him on with open arms and loud cheering.

The boy squeezes his hands, encouraging him gently, "Don't worry. This time, I'll be there to catch you when you fall." He turns around, looking at the total darkness of the room. No hesitation. No lingering regret. This is the moment he's been waiting for. Illusion and reality merge into one. He smiles the smile of defeat when the nurse rushes in, and as her hands reach out to grab him, he jumps.

"I will fall."

In the night garden, a secret flower is just blooming
Has someone just passed by my weary life?
Sometimes I can't help but think
The hundreds of graves are still here, crying
Our life seems to have no other new desire
And I have been living on fever dreams.
I have closed my heart, far too many times
Only to kneel by my bleeding wounds
Because you have taken my sincerest prayers
And left me in this quiet solitude on life's roadside—

Is It True

"Is it true what they say about you?"

The interviewer sits opposite him and pushes ever so lightly on the start button of the voice recorder. He can almost hear the sound of his index finger on the plastic material. He wonders if it is the right thing to come here so soon after learning about the murder. He needs a sensational headline for the newspaper, and whatever he can get out of this murderer's mouth, it will be a gold mine for the editor-in-chief. But looking at the haggard face in front of him, with the sunken cheeks, the unkempt beard, the darkened eyes, and the twisted lips, the interviewer has a sudden sense that he is stepping into an unknown land. An uncharted territory, full of barbed wire fences, wildly grown thistles, and weeds. There is something about the murderer's eyes that makes the interviewer shudder— not with fear but with a bad premonition, a strange feeling that he's been caught inside a trap without an opening for escape— and he taps the pen on the table incessantly, trying to drive away the wildest thoughts. The eyes that no longer shine. The lifeless body, trying its best to imitate what a human could be.

"What do they say about me?" the murderer asks. His hands are both cuffed on the table. He smiles with a raspy breath; his beard trembles with the motion. He is too old for this. After all, he is always too old for everything that happens to him.

"Well, they say your love never lasts." The interviewer taps his pen on the notepad. The sound in the silent room is unnerving to him. It reminds him too much of the sound of those fingers in a distant past, tapping on the window glass in the rain. There was once a man in his life who would run through miles of stormy road with him just to capture the first morning light on a muddy dune, laughing about the dirt on their boots, proving with the heat of his body and the beating of his heart that there is more to this life than an empty article and a click-bait title. But that is not the point. He feels the word form on his tongue, each letter dancing on his lips as he silently draws it out: love.

"Do you suppose that love, anyone's love, any type of love, will last?"

"I don't know." The interviewer exhales. He is exhausted by the long drive and the seemingly longer conversation he is about to have. Perhaps it was not the right decision to come here after all. Why did he think he would be the right person to take on this case? He is far too inexperienced. He writes good articles; anyone in his department can tell him that. But everyone will also inflict on him that same wounding look of ridicule and mockery. "You write pathetically melodramatic." And he knows they are right. He doesn't focus on the story. He is too busy digging up the wounds that remain. But there once was a man who would understand.

He closes his eyes, forcing himself to stay in the present. *Temptation, thou art a heartless bitch.*

His eyes trace the figure of the inmate. An old man; not so much because of age but because of the solitude within these four walls. The unkempt beard has grown thicker than the blood on his fingers. His hair has grown thinner than the life he took. He remembers seeing the crime scene photos. A crime of passion. The young boy lay face-down with a rope around his neck, his eyes wide with terror, his mouth hanging, his fingers clawing at his throat. One will assume that he had tried, till the very end, to cling onto life. He yearned to live with a fire that was yet to be distinguished in those lusterless eyes, and that was what made the crime more heinous. The victim was twenty years old. But the death in those photos did not fascinate the interviewer as much as the mug shot of the criminal at that time. A 35-year-old man, smiling into the camera, tears streaming down his face, as he held onto the name tag. Sadness and beauty, caught within a single frame. If it were not for the terrible event, that might have been the photo to win a prize.

"I suppose it doesn't," the interviewer says, rubbing his eyebrows, wondering for what reason he has come all the way here to this prison. "Do you suppose it does?" he asks, for conversation's sake.

"I don't suppose anything," the old man says with a loud cackle, then he coughs, convulsing, trying to catch his breath, "I know it doesn't."

"Is that why you killed him? At a time when the act of sodomy can lead to jail time and execution, what gave you the courage to fall in love with a man, and then, what gave you the courage to kill him?"

"You would be surprised. What if I told you that what gave me the courage to fall in love with him was the courage that I used to kill him?"

"And what was it?" The interviewer perks up. This might be the gold mine he is chasing after. He picks up the pen, ready to jot down the motives, the ugly, hidden truth of a human's nasty nature, the gruesome murder scene, picturing in his head multiple, tentative headlines. Among them, "Gay man of XX years old killed because society forced him" and all the rest. But he could never have been prepared for what comes after.

"He was a human, Mr. Interviewer; he was a human. And as with any human, he knew all the tricks to cheat, to lie, to betray. But at the same time, he found in himself the power to love, to caress with the touch of a feather, to treasure things as if they were his last possession. He was the wickedest demon, and he was the holiest saint. He was the trash you throw away and he was the diamond ring you find in a dumpster on a rainy day."

"Well, it seems you were quite infatuated with him." The interviewer drops the pen, downcast.

This is not what he wants to hear. But nothing that comes out of this murderer will ever be what he wants to hear. He clutches the recorder, ready to stop the session. The inmate lowers his head and fumbles with his rough fingers. He seems to be finding his way out through Ariadne's thread on his palms, carved out so beautifully with so many scars, so many lines of hardship and suffering. So much pain.

"Listen, boy, if you're going to tell my story, tell it true. Don't fool the readers with beautiful words. Don't lie to them with make-believe details, with all the assumptions and suspicions. Just tell it true. Tell it as it has always been."

"Alright," the interviewer says, tapping his pen against the notepad, not intending to write down anything soon. He knows that no reader will buy a true story. He knows that the audience wants a shock, a glamorous love affair that ended in a bloody vengeance, and to top it off, a vicious blame to the injustice of society. He knows it all and yet, if only the readers could see this old man here, half of his face buried in darkness, the other half with a gentle lift at the corner of his mouth. Eyes for a lover, as the old people of the fading generation who still believe in the miracle of love would describe. This old man always has eyes for his lover. No matter how long it has been, no matter how time is supposed to kill every fiber of memory, his eyes are always there, watching the smile of his young lover as he taps his fingers on the window glass on a rainy day.

"So you were infatuated with him," the interviewer repeats in monotone.

"No, not 'infatuated.' Infatuation will quickly burn out as soon as you find another subject to aim for. This is not a simple infatuation. This is the demon. The demon called Love."

"So you loved him."

"Because he was a human."

"If it were any other human, would you be able to love them?"

"No. Perhaps in another lifetime, yes. But in this lifetime, no."

"Only him?"

"Only him."

"You might have been able to move on when you found out he cheated on you. Why kill him?"

"Because I am human."

"You make it hard to understand." The interviewer scratches his head. A familiar voice echoes from the past, calling his name with tenderness and warmth, but he suffuses it. He does not want to give in to temptation. Not now. Not ever.

"You're reading into the mind of a killer. You must be sure not to fall into the same trap. The same darkness. When you stare into the abyss," the murderer mumbles under his breath,

"the abyss stares back into you."

"Now, back to the story. You loved him because he was a human and you killed him because you are a human. Can you elaborate?" the interviewer snaps. He has no time for philosophical debates. Is it too late to back out now? The more he looks at the murderer, the more that figure of the past comes back to him, in all his glory and cruel brightness.

"Because a human can't possess a human," the murderer exhales a soft breath.

"And?"

"Take an example. When I like a teapot set, I buy it. I might break it, I might lose it, but I know that I always possess it. It won't run away. It won't turn on me. But when you love a human, how do you ever move on from that? A human will always leave you in the end."

"People love. People betray. People move on. Love doesn't excuse you from…" The interviewer rises from his seat. "This is madness."

"Did I ever say that as an excuse? You asked me what my motive was. I simply told you what it was to me. I don't care what you take from that."

"But if it were because he left—"

"It was not because he left. It was because he promised me that he would never leave. And I fucking believed it."

The inmate breaks down. His shoulders hunch over the table. His knuckles turn white from the sheer force. The scars where he was abused now become more visible to the interviewer's eyes under the glaring light of the room.

"He had promised me that he would never leave. And I always believed it. Through the beating, the burns of the cigarettes, the insults, the cuts, the slaps, the constant sex that almost felt like rape, I always believed it. I tolerated it all, with the thought that, if only he would love me. A little love would be enough."

"Was hoping the worst part?" the interviewer asks, more sympathetic now as he settles down in his seat.

"No. No. The wort part was, I foolishly put my absolute faith in a human's promise. I believed in intangible words. I believed in the existence of something that was nonexistent from the start."

"You killed him over a simple promise?"

"No, you don't understand. I killed him because he was more of a human than I ever was. If he were less of a human, perhaps his promises would be true. Perhaps his fingers would always calm the pain of my scars. Perhaps his smiles would always be the only light shining through my maze of sorrows, leading me out, bringing me home. And perhaps—perhaps his apologies would hurt less, just a little bit less."

"But aren't you a human?"

The inmate looks at him and smiles, tears streaming down his face; he has the same emotions from the mug shot all those years ago. If he had a camera with him, the interviewer would snap a photo. The decaying angel, he would title his piece. But he jerks out of his daydream. There is no angel here; they are all human. All too human.

"Love touched me on the shoulders. It killed my angel and empowered my demon. And when love touches you on the shoulders like that, you are no longer human."

"You know what? If you hadn't killed him, you'd still have your freedom. And you might recover from that."

"From what? From not being human? Can you tell me, then, Mr. Interviewer, how do you ever recover from not being human?"

The interviewer twists his pen in frustration. Love never

touches him on the shoulders; even if it did, he would not want it. He treasures being human. He treasures the ability to cheat, to lie, and to share half of what love is despite it all. Of all the commandments, the only thing he can obey is not to kill.

"Last question. If you were given the chance to go back in time, what would you choose? To kill or not to kill?"

"I won't answer that."

"Why?"

"Because the answer is not what you want to hear."

"I thought you wanted me to tell the truth?"

"And I believe both of us have seen what an ugly, grotesque, cruel, and monstrous creature the truth is. And I believe if it were your choice, the truth would be the first thing you killed. The first casualty."

"If it were me, I'd choose not to kill," the interviewer says, firm and determined.

"And if it were me, I'd choose not to publish this story."

"You know, I treasure freedom, and I always will," the interviewer says in lieu of a goodbye.

"Then, Mr. Interviewer, I hope love will never touch your shoulders."

The interviewer turns off the recorder, gathers his notepad and pen, and walks out. He thinks about the fresh air outside, the meals of the restaurants along the main boulevard, and the faraway countries on the Eastern hemisphere. He looks at his empty notepad with barely a word on it. Perhaps his editors won't like the result of this interview. His performance will suffer. His article won't be the kind of sensational headline he wishes it to be. The department will have a new piece of gossip by the water cooler. Look at him, the outcast, the failure, the melodramatic writer, chasing after wounds and digging up dead sufferers; he has failed again. They will laugh, they will mock, they will judge him with undisguised contempt in their eyes, faking their smiles, saying he will fare better next time. But they can't buy what he's gotten in his hands, and boy, isn't that fresh air so delicious?

The inmate is led back to his cell. *It's amazing how simple bricks and walls can separate the life we lead*, the interviewer thinks as he trods down the pavement to the bus stop, waiting for his turn to leave this forsaken prison, perhaps forever. The past comes back and perches on his shoulders. He once knew a man who would share this agony, this smoldering desire to break down and cry that he, too, wants to burn in the blazing flame of love and other demons. That man would smile at him, telling him that it is all nonsense. That he should never believe the fever dream of "us against the world" could possess such strong power. The interviewer takes a deep breath, caving to temptation at last. What does it matter? The man in his past is dead. Before the interviewer had the chance to taste what love was, it slipped through his fingers, disintegrated into a million pieces of memory. The murderer is right; nothing is going to last.

Many years later, the interviewer might not find that love, the kind of love the inmate has spoken of. But because he is a human, and humans have survived thus far, outlived all the creatures that ever existed on this earth, he lights a candle and hopes that when that demon touches his shoulders, he will survive it, too.

The Hunger, Or What Love Could Have Been

First, she is the mountain.

She rumbles and erupts a volcano occasionally, when the mood strikes her, or when the earth moves her enough to burst. She is smoldering with lava inside her heart. Black with burned charcoal and unexplored caves, she yearns to be understood. She welcomes everyone and anyone with open arms, happy when they land the first footstep on her bosom and happier still when they leave the last footstep on her body. *The strangers,* she thinks, *who come by, not unfrequently, to take my bounty, who leave as soon as they are fed, who never let a chance of winning escape, the greed in their eyes, the vanity in their words, the empty promises echoing through the abysses and the forests—but aren't they beautiful in their deceit?* And she loves them for it. It is in her nature to love humanity.

And she remains a mountain, until the last rock on her slope is removed, for science's purpose, for the humans she loves so much to move forward, to advance, to chase after the lives they want. She remains a mountain when the first bomb destroys her caves, when the last innovation of her beloved humanity kills another set of her beloved humanity; when the drills get in, when the gold gets out, when the crystals are sold, and the lava no longer holds any value, she stands tall, bares her flesh for them to take, rob, and ravage. She remains a mountain until what is left of her is a pile of barely recognizable rocks and pebbles. The trees are long gone. The forests are burned. The caves are sunken in. She cannot recognize herself. Is this how she's always been? Where is the anger? Where is the volcano? Where is the rumble? She chases after the footsteps of the last human who is trying to excavate a crystal from her bosom. "Don't leave," she asks. "Don't walk away from me," she begs. The man looks at her, barely any emotion on his face, and he answers her plea with a simple, "Yeah, this mountain no longer has any value." In the dark, no one can hear the mountain shatter.

First, he is the earth.

He lies beneath the mountain, watching her laugh. He admires her glorious beauty, the way the sunlight dances on her face, the way the wind caresses the canopies of trees in her forest. He lies there, silently listening to her talking about the humans who keep barging in and leaving right after. He never shares her adoration for them. The strangers, he once told her, they are the reincarnation of sin. They will take and take and take, and in their sweeping greed, they will destroy everything you possess. But his words fall on deaf ears. So he watches her every day as her rocks are removed, her trees felled, her cave destroyed, for the sake of the humanity she loves so dearly, more than what he can ever be in her eyes.

She never knows what he hides beneath the surface. The detonation of the explosives that would cause blood to soak him, corpses to pile on him, decaying flesh to spill on him. She never knows the filthy history her humans force him to swallow, the defeats as well as the victories. She never knows the winners and the losers are both despised, and before she can make another rumble, before she can erupt another volcano, a war has already started. He witnesses them dying, killing, feasting on the other's bounty, and all the while, it keeps occurring to him, *That will be her fate. My fate. Our fate.* The system keeps grinding. He has no power to stop it. He only wishes she could open her eyes to the monstrosity that is happening. "Look," he wants to scream to her as the humans keep bombing her caves. "Look at them. The children are dying." But he can't. What he tolerates, what pains he carries, he embraces them alone.

That is why, when she shatters in the dark, no one can hear the earth howl the last mournful song.

Then, she becomes wood.

She places herself in the course of humanity's development. She is in the first building, and she will remain there until the last one falls. She has never imagined a life so bright. As she burns in the stove, the crackling sound of flame echoing in her ears, she listens to the fairy tales of old. The princesses, the witches, the happily-ever-after, and all those creations that humans use to soothe the innocent hearts of the yet-to-be-wounded children—she loves them more than whatever life can offer. Sometimes, when she lies there in the dark silence, she dreams about the little mermaid. She wonders why the prince doesn't recognize his beloved salvation, and why he doesn't love the poor girl, who had paid her life to buy a second of being by his side. She wonders why the witches are cruel to the beauty, and why the beasts are hated. She knows the beasts—they are her friends, and they are easily misunderstood. They don't have a human's look, but they have as much of a human's heart as any person. She wonders still if the princesses are what they appear to be: kindhearted, gentle, and always stretching out their beautiful, slender hands, decorated with gemstones and glittering gold, to the poor and the helpless. She lives her life in blissful dreams. Some are filled with stories; some are filled with imagination: what could her life be if she could become human? She thinks of the dances, the magnificent balls, and the lights shining on her face as she dances in the arms of the charming prince she loves, who would love her for who she is, who never cares about beauty, appearances, rich or poor, or whether she has a fish tail instead of feet.

And as the flame burns, she witnesses the changes. The humans she lives with no longer tell fairy tales by the fireplace. They wear a haggard look on their face. Their dresses tatter and are full of holes. The children grow old, and they no longer hold sparkling eyes, wishing for a night ball with the marvelous prince waiting somewhere in a faraway palace. Those places are never there. Reality settles in. Arguments begin. Instead of make-believe stories, she now hears the breaking of dishes on the floor, the screaming, the shouting, the constant crying, saying they wish each other was dead. She looks on in horror as the children she once loved now reach for the vases, the bowls, the pots and pans—whatever items are still in the house, not yet pawned—and throw them to the set of adults who used to cradle them in their embrace when they were plagued with nightmares and imaginary ghosts.

She wonders if it is true that no love will ever stand the test of time. She sees the mother weep silently in the night, bruises on her face, deep cuts on her wrists. She wishes she could alleviate the pain in her life, but how can a stick of wood do anything to shoulder the burden no human could bear? She sits there, listening to the silent sobs, thinking of the life this woman could have led if love had not been there. Doubts rise in her heart. It is not supposed to be like this. The princess is supposed to live happily ever after with the prince. The children are supposed to laugh and cherish every moment they have with their parents. Why is this mother here, all alone, desperate and cold, with no one to lean on? *If love hurts this much,* she thinks, *isn't it better to not love at all?*

The answer comes to her, too clear and too cruel, that morning, when the mother she sympathizes with takes her in her hand and strikes the drunken husband twenty-four times on the head. As she lies there in the pool of blood, witnessing the woman taking her own life with the kitchen knife, a wistful smile on her face, she finally realizes humans are not as strong as she thought they were. They always succumb to temptation, and they always let love and its roster of demons win.

He becomes the fire.

He swears with his life at stake that with his power, this time, he will protect her. But he never expects her to be wood. Watching her wince and cry with pain as humans toss her in his arms, he feels his existence break away into nothingness. But every time he extinguishes himself, the humans bring him back. He lives only to watch her being tortured. She dies only to fuel and prolong his life further. When he thinks he can't bear this pain anymore, he realizes she never grudges him, or them, or any higher authority, for this. She relishes the fact that she is still here, on this plane of existence, with the humans she loves so much. Through her suffering, she would listen with rapture to the fairy tales and the happy endings of the stories he knows are just lies to appease the hunger of an innocent heart. So he lingers on, his last breath licking at her open wounds, trying to get closer, to convey to her that he never loves this arduous toil and that she is the only reason he survives.

He hears the arguments. He sees the beatings, the cuts, the bruises, the tattered dresses, the children abusing their parents. Isn't this what he has known for far too long? He has seen how humans have destroyed, and he should have known their cruelty knows no bounds. But he has never seen a woman cry. That night, as he witnesses the glimmering tears trickle down the bruised cheeks of the mother, he feels his heart ache back to life. He wants to reach out his hand to touch her, but all he ever does is hurt. He wants to soothe her, but he roars instead. His voice is monstrous even to his own ears, and the woman keeps shedding unending tears. He realizes what little power he holds in his hands, that even if humans can wage a million wars, what they can never do is soothe the pain of this worn-out mother in her threadbare dress. He stares, wonder in his eyes. He never knew love could hurt so much and still be so bright. He wants to hold her in his arms and tell her that even though it is cruel, he never wants to let her go.

But that morning, after the woman kills her husband and commits suicide, the woodreturns to him, saying, "I give up on love."

"But you love humans," he says, trying to hide the hurt, but the hurt never leaves.

"Humans, what do they matter? They're so fragile that they will end up killing each other," she says, her eyes slowly fading away.

"But love is all I have to offer." He reaches out, trying to catch her in his arms.

"And it never amounts to much, does it? After all, you are also a stranger."

She breaks into pieces of dust. He roars for the last time—no one knows if it is laughter or tears—and extinguishes into the nothingness from where he has come.

Then she is born to this earth as a woman, living a woman's life.

She spends her life sitting in a discreet corner of a worn-out, quiet cafe, watching people pass her by. She doesn't love them anymore. *The strangers*, she thinks, *they come and they leave. Forever and always will they be strangers.* But something inside her still burns. The remnant of the undying, unyielding embers. She watches them smolder, waiting for them to waste away, no longer expecting them to help her through the loneliest days. She learns that there is no joy in being human. She tries seizing the day, but she is no longer the mountain, or a piece of wood. She knows that there is as much bravado in letting go as in holding on. She sees people cry in their desperate hours, only to smile through their suffering the next. All the while, she wonders, what for? She's been in the rat race for longer than she can remember. She realizes though a human's life is short, it feels almost immortal. An eternity buried under the carefully measured sand of the hourglass. And yet, she is still sitting there, stirring the bitter, black coffee, waiting for hope to touch her shoulders again. To understand why she chooses to live, no matter the cost.

He comes to see her one of those days, when the sadness is slanting through the descending twilight of the remaining of day, when she thinks that she is born to witness to the cruel twist of fate, or something as flamboyant as that. He comes by and sits opposite her, ordering the same strong, black coffee, not looking her in the eyes, not asking whether she wants him there or not. He comes and he stays, binding his life to the chair, under her scrutiny. Her eyes trace his face, the soft features and the determined eyes, with a sharp gaze, almost bordering on too fierce to be human. He picks up the spoon, his slender fingers entwining around the bland object, seeming unaffected by her cold, indifferent stare. But his tremor betrays whatever scorching feeling lies beneath his facade. He chances a glance at her face, and she says, half in mockery, half in earnest, "Your face looks familiar."

"I don't think I've ever met you before, or else…" he replies, taking a sip from the cold cup.

"Or else?"

"Or else I would've remembered."

"Really? Why?" she muses. Finally, life has become interesting to her, and she dares not think too far ahead, like imagining how this will end.

"Because it's hard to forget a face that would cause you so much pain," he says, lifting the cup to his lips again in the span of ten seconds, his fingers still trembling.

"I haven't caused you pain."

"You already did. And the most painful thing of all, you don't care enough to remember."

"You talk as if you've known me for a very long time."

"And a very long time it is, indeed."

"Where have I seen you?"

"You haven't seen me. You never did. But I've seen you. Not meeting you face to face. Not this close. Never this close. But I've seen you."

"When?"

"Since the time of old. Since the first mountain was erected on earth. Since the Word."

"You are enigmatic."

"It doesn't help."

"You think that is a compliment."

"No, I don't. But if you want me to think it is, I'm willing to."

"What's your deal?"

"Nothing. I just want to be here," he says, finally looking her in the eyes as a strange, dark emotion rages in his bottomless irises. "I just want to stay."

She leans back, focusing on the people passing on the busy road. Somehow, she knows he will leave. But for the first time in her limited life, she feels the spark of an unfamiliar fire, a different kind of pain. It is small in the beginning; then it grows. Burning through the forests and the lands; the heavy, ripened rice stalks and the bamboo groves; the immovable rocks and the hills of green grass. She watches as it becomes her whole existence. And yet, it is greedy. It keeps growing, larger than what her body can contain. It spills out of her skin, pouring out of her mouth, until she is drowning in its bosom. She learns that it is hope. And worse still, or better still, she learns that hope could kill, on the day she starts expecting the man to come back and sit opposite her, just like the day he first walked into her life. She expects always, knowing that life can only offer her a fleeting, temporary act.

"Hey," he says by way of greeting, "You're still here."

"It seems you expect otherwise."

"No. No, on the contrary. I... I hoped you would still be here, in a way."

"In a way."

"Things never turn out the way I expect so I learn to never expect much."

"Out of life?"

"Out of anything."

"That's defeatism."

"It's my only chance at winning."

"You're weird."

"Will it make you remember me?" He smiles, his eyes twinkling. He stops pretending to be the cold, toxic, masculine man she first saw. And she doesn't know since when, but he has abandoned the strong, black coffee, opting for the sickeningly sweet chocolate frappuccino drink with a thick layer of whipped cream on top.

"I don't think there is anything to remember or to forget here," she says, but in her mind, she is carving his features into imaginary stone, treasuring every detail, every line, as if he is the last person on earth.

"Then it seems I'm still failing."

"In what?"

"A race."

"A rat race? Please, spare me the empty, vainglorious symbolism and irony." She scoffs, sipping on the coffee he detests so much.

"No, a race of my own." He smiles ruefully. "But I guess it is empty and vainglorious symbolism all the same."

"Don't do that."

"Do what?"

"That." She points generally at his face. "Sadness is not becoming of you, and your sadness is wasted on me. I'm never known as someone who would care."

"It's funny." He fiddles with the straw. "Because I know you would. You always would. You just, if I am permitted to say, give up. Because of humanity's stark cruelty on one dark night, you decided to give up."

"You tell such pretty stories."

"I don't tell them. I don't even have the talent to fabricate them. I only try to see humans through your eyes."

"And are you successful? Doing that?"

"No." He laughs, bitter and dour. "I never was. Never will be. You have the bounty of which I have none."

"Love?"

"Forgiveness."

He stares at her, his eyes glistening. Though there are no tears, she can't help but hear his silent cry echo in the darkening cafe. The sky is littered with a million stars, shining through their deaths. That should be the sign for her to stop hoping, but she persists. Perhaps he is right; she has a bounty that he has not. A bounty of a fool. A bounty no one will want, because everyone would be better off without it. She seizes the table's edge, feeling a rage rising within her bosom. She knows it is never easy, but no one tells her about the pain of the aftermath. Where is her bravado when she needs it the most? She closes her eyes, exhales, and drops her hands by her sides. Of course, what can she expect? She is only a human.

"Don't talk about me as if you know me the most." She breathes softly.

"I never intended to do that. I only want to…"

"You want to?" she probes.

"I want to tell you how beautiful you were."

"And now I am not?"

"You still are," he says, never breaking the intense eye contact, never taking away the unhidden longing in his burning gaze. "But you're running away from it. You're running away from yourself, from what you were, from what you could be. And if only I could show you how magnificent your beauty reigns on earth, how it rules me, I would pay with my life. Yes, if only."

"Empty words and empty promises," she mocks. Her voice

is soft, but the cut is deep on his bleeding heart, and she can see it in those deep, mournful eyes. "You would do better than thinking that I'll believe them."

He never says a word. His fingers tap on the table to no rhythm at all. His eyes close. He is listening to sorrowful songs, decades old, playing on repeat in the cafe. Whether he is enjoying the dreary melody or simply drowning her existence, she doesn't know. But she understands the pain on his face as he lowers his head, letting a faint shadow of a stranger passing by on the road outside cast over his eyes, disguising a tear streaming down his cheek. She detects the fading glimmer of the drop as it drips onto the tabletop, and in the silence of the cafe's soft piano sonatas, she can hear the sadness talk. How much loneliness can a human bear? And she wonders, partly in stupefied amazement, partly in guilty conscience, whether she is the cause of it all: the pain he suffers, the yearning in his eyes, the longing in his voice, and the expectation he sometimes shows, palpitating in his breath. She clutches her heart, wishing it to stop before the seed of hope strangles it to death.

But she watches the flame burn. She lets it consume whatever is still left of her, thinking it is a deserving end. Perhaps this is what it means to live, or perhaps this is what it means to be killed softly. She will figure it out when her time comes. For now, she just observes this statuesque melancholy in front of her, oblivious to the passage of time, of things changing, of people leaving, and immerses herself in the wistful thinking of what could have been. She doesn't believe in magic. She knows it takes more than a spell and a flimsy belief to fix a broken ocean. She thinks about the tale of Moses, about the people the prophet saves by telling them to blindly keep faith in an entity no one before him could prove and no one after him could succeed in bringing back to life. Then she lingers on the last note in the man's words, the subdued tone, the meek smile, the downcast gaze under the quivering eyelashes: *If only*.

She laughs derisively in a raging self-mockery. She detests those words. *If only*. There's no "if" in her life. It's either doing it and regretting it or never doing it and regretting it anyway. She looks on the man's words as a mirage, a make-believe scenario, where he's trying to show her that the grass is indeed greener, and she can't see it because she is wearing a pair of deeply rose-tinted glasses. She presumes, and she hates that she is presuming, because it lets her know that she cares more about his opinion, his thoughts, his ideas, his existence, than the mass of grey people passing through out there, walled off from her by a thin window. It lets her know that she is losing, and her escape route is slowly breaking away. She stares at him, trying to detect from his countenance a vulnerability that she can weaponize, something she can use to defend herself, to protect her from the stab that she is sure he will inflict on her, not now, but sometime in the future. Yet, all she can glimpse from his haggard face and his hollow cheeks is a surge of glowing, smoldering agony. It is so sweet, so tantalizing, and so akin to the thing she has lost. *Love*, she thinks, *that is the one thing I don't have in bounty*.

"If you look at me so intensely, I will get the wrong idea," the man says without looking at her.

"What idea?"

"The one idea that will kill anyone."

"Such as?"

"Did you ever hear about Hans Christian Andersen and his story, 'The Little Mermaid'?"

"I heard about 'The Little Mermaid.' Heard plenty of it. Far too much, I'd say."

"Did you know that it was based on his unrequited love for his male lover when the latter got married?"

"And?"

"I don't know. Sometimes, I can't help but think of it."

"You will spend a whole day thinking of the story."

"No, I only think about Hans Christian Andersen. About how much pain he had to suffer to produce such a devastating story."

"Perhaps it has a happy ending, in its own way."

"You think so?"

"It doesn't matter what I think, does it?" She tries to smile, but it's hard. Every attempt to be indifferent grows harder the more she talks to him. "The prince and the princess are happy. Perhaps that's the point of the story. Perhaps that's what Hans Christian Andersen believed."

"And is that what you believe?" His voice doesn't hide his straightforward consternation. He stares at her, the same fierce gaze, the same embers. His being is the fire. And her existence is wood. She feels parched. Her throat is dried with a thirst she never knew she was capable of.

"Whether I believe in it or not..." She fumbles with words and fidgets with her hands, betraying her otherwise calm demeanor. "The story won't change. The little mermaid always dies in the end."

"Will that make you happy? Is that what eases your conscience at night?"

"Why do you care?"

"Because that's not what you should do." He slams his fist on the table, jerking up from his chair. A fury never before seen illuminates his face as he yells, "One Hans Christian Andersen or a million Hans Christian Andersens won't define what your life should be, or what you should believe. Why should we succumb to others' thoughts and ideas, when you have more than they can offer? You have your life, and your life is perfect. The little mermaid might have died in the end because Hans Christian Andersen decided so, but this is your life, and in your life, no mermaid has to die. Don't you see it? Don't you see the power you hold in your hands? Why, oh why, must you give up?"

He breaks down, collapsing on the table like a pile of baked earth after the rain, broken in between and broken everywhere. He thinks he has lost all hope, all expectation, but the pain is real. He is standing still, rooted to the tiled floor of the old cafe, a vessel, empty of soul and essence, watching the remnants of himself thrashing on the ground, begging her, *Won't you give me some love?* But he knows better than to utter the first pleading word. He feels small, his entire existence reduced to the next beating of her heart. There are a million words he wants to say. *Better words*, he thinks. Better chance of getting her to glance at him for a fleeting second, he dreams. He can never figure out what lies beneath her skin, the layer of emotionless tissues and muscles that seem incapable of moving but are still strong enough to instill a towering fear inside him, ready to crash down, ready to fall. So he sits. The greater the love grows, the more heinous the fear becomes, and in the middle of it, without him knowing, realizing, seeing it for himself, he turns into a coward.

She avoids his destruction, avoids witnessing his tall figure cascading down the chair, avoids the humanity in him being destroyed. Instead, she turns her head to look out the windows, busying herself with watching other people living another kind of life. In her mind, she draws a thousand simulations, each with its own suitable ending. None of them has a happy ending for the little mermaid. All of them has a jackass like Hans Christian Andersen to fuck it up badly enough so she can stay away from the hurt for good. She wonders what will become of her after her limited time ends. The sand of the hourglass is still running. She can only enjoy it here, knowing that time is still on her side. But is this all life has to offer? And is this what they call living? Is she a real human being, or is she just pretending? Watching the light dim on the pavement, she realizes she doesn't know much. About people. About love. About life. About him. She is acting a fool's role, thinking she is the queen ruling a massive kingdom of darkness. What if she had a different belief? And what if the man is right? Tapping her fingers on the table, she hums quietly to the melody of the song in the dark cafe, thinking, *I'll entertain it, the "If only,"* and in the quietude of her soul, she can hear the soft laughter of hope.

"I have intruded upon your solitude," he says, his hands up in the air. "I imposed my belief on you. I was wrong. I don't know what you've been through."

"Neither do I." She smiles, her eyes glinting with something familiar to him, something that makes his heart jump, racing to the finish line far too fast, far too early—something like kindness for pure kindness's sake.

"But I have no right."

"And I have no reason to be angry with you."

"You should."

"Do what?"

"Get angry. With me. With anyone, for that matter. You know what? Hatred, in a way, is also proof that we are living with a beating heart. A ferocious heart at that." He laughs.

"Define *ferocious*," she muses, chasing after the echo of his laughter in the night.

"Well, like passion."

"Define *passion*."

"Like lighting a house on fire."

"Like throwing wood to build a flame."

"Like knowing that you have only this one time on earth. Never more. Never again."

"Like forgiveness."

"Like love."

She chuckles, then bursts out laughing until tears start streaming down her face. Or at least, she thinks she is laughing, but in his eyes, she is shedding the tears of all the life she has ever held dear in her embrace. He knows he shouldn't have these feelings, but he is glad. A part of him still wants to believe—naively, though—that the embers are yet to die, and his time hasn't finished like a niente at the end of beautifully written diminuendo. He waits, feeling every nerve in his body grow taut to the point of tearing. *A word*, his eyes try to tell her, *just a word from you, and this will be worth every suffering I've been through, every suffering I will bear, and all things in between.* In the hanging silence of the cafe, as the last client is leaving, he can hear his own breathing reverberating against the walls, the copper decorations, the cups and the spoons on the shelves. He waits until he can't take it anymore, and as he begins to hyperventilate in the sudden surge of a panic attack, she pushes herself up and releases him from the hell he is living in. "I'm going," she says.

"Wait," he says, his voice louder than he intends it to be. Nothing is ever as he intends it to be. "You're not going to stay?"

"You know how things go. People come and people leave. I've given you so many opportunities. You should've taken the chance the first time around." She smiles. "Since it has come to this dress rehearsal drag, I'll be leaving."

"Don't be a stranger." He feels the plea desperate in his tremulous words. What has been left of hope?

"No, I'm not. Darling, it's you." She picks up her coat, tying up her loose hair, pushing her chair in, and flashing him a final smile like the last mercy she will ever bestow on anyone. "You are the stranger."

With those words, she walks out the door, never once turning back to see the life she has broken. It happened exactly as he had feared. He can't say that he is surprised by the outcome. After all, he's seen this ending so many times it has become almost an old friend. A bitter one, but it still makes a good companion along the road, nonetheless. He pushes the sweet chocolate drink away, half finished. The music enters its diminuendo, fading into nothingness. He stays there, staring out the windows, trying to find her figure among other people passing by on the moonlit pavement. Other strangers.

She finds enough strength to leave because she loves in her womanly way. Too bad he was born a man, and he can only see her love through a man's lens.

He was born as a human.

He sits there in the dark cafe, looking out at the people passing by, wondering what has become of his dreams and what his hopes were. He starts losing sight of them the moment he opens his eyes and realizes that he has given in to the divine comedy, that he willingly acted out a role on the theatrical stage, only to have another glimpse at her shadow as she danced away in the descending darkness of the act's crescendo. He thinks about the word *sacrifice* and its meaning, or lack of meaning. He thinks about the give-and-take nature of the words, about how human beings bestow on each letter the most beautiful and tragic heroism to justify the wrongs they had done. About the world and how it is seen from the wheel of history, from the eyes of the winners and the defeated. The vainglorious act of living and taking life for granted, thinking that things will remain there for eternity, but humanity won't last. He leans back on his seat, immersing himself in the emptiness of the stage. The costume is old. The role is ending. He might need to shed the skin to reveal another him within—stronger, more resilient, he hopes, so that he can withstand the final battle, the last great war, the loneliness and solitude of being the only living person on earth, since the day she left.

He wishes, but he dares not utter it. He prays, but he silences the words. He hopes, expecting all hopes to fail. He dreams, knowing dreams won't come true. He lives a life borrowed from the many lives he's seen through the windows. He tries to feel their pain, to see their suffering and understand it as she would have understood it. He wants to get to the final reason, to explain to himself why she had loved human beings with so fervent a heart and had abandoned them with such cruel indifference. But all he finds are shards of broken glass, pieces of what people used to be before the world broke them apart, and he never recovers them from the breaking point. He wonders what beauty she had seen in those miseries, those relentless cries, hidden behind a dark veil of despair, void of any light and happiness. He wonders if she is drawn to them because in a mad moment of titillating passion, when the wind's caresses grow too soft and the cradle of the trees are no longer enough to withhold the burning fire of her soul, she finds the pain in their eyes and the sorrow in their tears sweet enough to die for, to yearn, to yield, to surrender. To kill herself over and over again so the human within them can live as cruelly and brightly as the day on which she lost sight of their beauty and sadness.

He wonders if she ever knows it herself, that she only loves them that much because she wants to be loved in the same way, in the same manner, with the same fervor. All that love he cannot give, because he never knows how to touch someone's shoulders with the lightness of hope and the grudging weight of expectations.

He looks at his reflection in the window's foggy glass. The weather has turned colder. The people walk faster, trying to move through life as they move through any other chore of their routine, with the same boredom and the same patient toleration, bordering on stoicism. She stopped returning to the cafe. But he still remains there, at the same place. He sits at the same table, the same chair, reserving the seat opposite him for the person he treasures the most in his world. His world is limited, a barbed wire, fenced-up world, but a world worth fighting for nonetheless. The lights are on, illuminating the scrunched-up noses and the wrinkled faces; all of them differ only in their degree of pain and suffering. He thinks back on the conversation he had with her and can't help but think he has hoped for the most improbable thing. She is naive in her agony, and he is not a wise man in his love when the first and only action he can think of to get her attention is standing there, watching her burn, hoping that one day, in her suffering for others' love, she will notice his pain.

He wonders if he wants her to come back. On the coldest

day, when the heater of the cafe is broken and the draft blows in, cutting his face with its sharp, icy blades, he allows himself the little pleasure of wondering what he will do, what he will say, if she decides to come back here, to walk through that door, as naturally and nonchalantly as the day she walked away. He pictures her sitting opposite him, smiling softly, too soft to be her old self, but it would be enough to release him from the hell he is living in. Sacrifice, he will say to her, is the most selfish thing a human can ever do for another human.

He was born into suffering as much as any other human. He never cares to alleviate the hurt. He takes it as a sign that he is alive. Each breath fills his lungs with fire, and each day, when he opens his eyes, he fears the road that lays ahead of him, and the road behind. But he walks on. He knows the choice will be there—the choice of giving up. And he never ceases to be astounded when he lies in his bed at night, fully awake, realizing that he has survived. He is still standing strong where many before him have tried and failed. He is still moving on, dragging the shackles on his legs, where many are lying there, breathless, dead. There are times—more often than he wants to admit—when he stops to take a break and glances around him, counting the people who still remain there, who still persevere no matter what. People like him, who lean on the shadow of the night, find comfort and consolation in their own solitude. But each time, he realizes they are less and less. One day, he wakes up, and in the flooding light of the morning, he finally understands that there is as much to fear in the dawn as there is in the darkness. Each has its own kind of monster; each bears its own curse.

He wonders if she thinks the same. He found her when life had left her enough wounds but had just inflicted on him the first pain. The moment he first saw her through the window of the cafe, he knew that it was worth being born. It was worth suffering this much just for this single moment of glory. But she never saw him. He could have been bleeding to death in front of her eyes; she wouldn't care to detect his last whisper, faintly ringing as his breath rattled. All he ever was, and ever could be in her eyes, was a man. He has a simple mind and always thinks straightforwardly. It is easy for him to hide his pain underneath a thick layer of smiles and laughter, hoping she wouldn't notice, longing for her to understand. He'd rather choose her indifference than the possibility of rejection. And all she ever was to him, all she ever will be, is the universe where his life is unfolding in excruciatingly poignant longing, wishful thinking, waiting with patience for him to pass through with the thought, *Yes, perhaps we were meant for each other*, like a blessing. He knows that life is not surviving or existing with her. Life is either to live to the fullest extreme or to never be here at all. So he hesitates. Faced with such strength and bravado, a mere human like him can only cower and bow in humiliation, wishing it was he who was the focal point of that love, that eternal source of the passion to live, to go on, to keep pushing against the dark side of the world. He thinks he is the flame, but the flame dies out. He presumes she is wood, but she is a forest fire, and in her eyes, that fierce light keeps burning, until all that is left of her is the barest soul, challenging the strongest amor of the weakest hero on earth, who possesses the armor of indifference.

He takes the jump, knowing his life will never be the same. She walks away, knowing her life will move forward in the way it always has. And he won't blame her for that, or for anything else.

It comes as a surprise, then, when one day, she walks back into the cafe, heads straight to the table, and takes her usual seat. She takes a book out, flipping through the pages, stopping at a bookmark in the shape of a cat's paw, focusing on the lines she has left. He waits, not breaking the pregnant silence between them, not disturbing the little moments of joy that are bursting in his stomach like summer fireworks. If it were possible, he would stop his own breathing. She seemingly doesn't notice any of his straining effort to remain as he is. Her fingers hover lightly over the page, her lips set into a sort of gentle smile, and she hums to herself the sad melody of the cafe. He wonders if she has seen him, if—whether somewhere between the day they parted and the day she returns—he has died a little each time the thought of her struck up in his mind, and now he is a ghost who cannot move on because of the bitter regret of an undying wish. He lingers there, his fingers gripping the table's edge. His drink has turned cold. He doesn't know since when, but he has changed from the sweet chocolate drink filled with whipped cream to the bitter black coffee that she likes, hoping to chase after the shadow she left behind, to taste the flavor of the life she had led before they met, to indulge himself in the tiny happiness of knowing that at least she and him share a link, though fragile and frayed. He is human in arduous love, and he breathes the feverish words, "That's an interesting bookmark you've got."

"What? Oh, the cat's paw?" she asks, not lifting her eyes from the page. She has stopped on that same page for a long time, and he knows he shouldn't, but he also knows that God listens, and God will excuse his delusion and his hope.

"The cat's paw. Yes."

"I think cats are selfish creatures."

"Do you like them?"

"Cats? Or selfish creatures?"

"Either one. Whatever tickles your fancy. I mean—"

"You mean the crazy person's choice, don't you?" She looks up from her book, a familiar twinkle of mischievousness in her eyes. He shifts in his seat, unable to calm the raging dreams in his mind. *Oh,* he thinks, *I need so little to live happily.*

"No, I mean, if you like them, I will like them. Anyway. In a sense. Or something along those lines."

"You know, there are enough copies out there. You can range them based on their degree of likeness and the quality of the materials. You can also categorize them into neat catalogs and shelve them. But what you can't, what you shouldn't, and what I hope you won't do, is to be another copy. At least, not a copy of me."

"Can I take that as a compliment?"

"Will it make any difference?" she asks, her voice monotonous, and it sets his nerves on edge again.

"It will. It makes a great difference. To me; not to you. But it will."

"Typical need for validation?"

"If you want to think so."

"Why do you care so much what I think or don't think?"

"Because I was assigned to the divine comedy, and my role is the fool."

She closes the book, puts it neatly on the table beside the hardly touched coffee, and leans forward to looks him straight in the eyes. He wonders if his answer is right or wrong, and whether there is any one true answer to solve the problem of everything. He wonders, at the same time, if she holds that answer close to her heart, if she plans on unleashing that monster when human beings least expect it, just for fun, or just for the sake of revenge, or worse still, if she never lets it out, and keeps it smoldering in her bosom, waiting until the day it finally swallows her whole. The cars outside race to their final destinations, though the people driving are yet to know where those places are. Some believe they are heading to heaven, walking through hell's gate. Some knowingly drive straight to that gate, hoping for the last redemption, the salvation of the higher indifference they call God. But he hopes and trusts in the benevolence of Him, the figment of imagination that is invoked whenever it is the most convenient for humans to lie, to cheat, to betray, to commit sin in the name of their holy faith, thinking it is goodness, and the Lord Almighty will forgive them all as He will come down to earth one of these days. He thinks it will take more than God's kindness—or any other deity's mercy, for that matter—to forgive the monstrous creation He has fashioned after His own image. Then he thinks of what the god's image would be like for mankind to be such a cruel, beautiful mess.

"It wouldn't work like that," she says, breaking his train of thought into tiny fragments of misshapen puzzle pieces.

"What wouldn't work?"

"Your way of thinking."

"You know what I was thinking?"

"I don't. But I can take a guess."

"I would be glad to hear your guess." He laughs, leaning back on his chair. "Is it very wild? Or is it extremely forgettable?"

She lifts her head, never averting her intense gaze, and he feels the forest fire spreading to his seat. He is burning slowly, and he knows she'd enjoy the pain on his face. "I can tell you my guess," she says, "and you can be the judge, whether it is forgettable, or wild, or anything in between."

"I'm listening."

"You think human beings are garbage."

"Not true," he says, a bit too hasty to hide his own astonishment.

"Yes, it shows in your eyes. You detest the passersby, the people outside, anything remotely human. You think they're cruel. You think they only beg for forgiveness when it is convenient for them to win a war. You think you're better than the rest of them, that they only believe in their makeshift faith, that they would use a fake reason to get what they want rather than hearing and protecting the truth. You think you understand enough about human nature to know there is no salvation for them. But you also think that a little love would be enough. You're naive in your sadness and melancholy. Do you know who you remind me of?"

"Who?" he asks, clenching his hands. His brain is on the edge of a bottomless abyss. He is right; she would understand his darkest thoughts. The hatred he dares not utter is the life she had lived through.

"You remind me of the person I once was. I was a lover. I was a dreamer. And I was once someone like you, a hopeless vagabond on the roadside, begging for the mercy of something I didn't know if I should believe in or not. But you know what?"

"What?"

"I had never been human. Not once."

She smiles at him. It is not happiness and there is no joy in her eyes. It looks more like a quiet acceptance of defeat. He falls at her feet, a million times over, just to witness the destruction of her soul. But she is resilient. She never yields, and even in her utmost defeat, she is still herself, vaingloriously beautiful.

She stands tall, her head straight, her face forward, and her eyes refuse to surrender, even when there is no hope left, when the chance of winning is less than a round, meaningless nothing. And it is in that moment that he realizes he has never understood anything about her. Since she was a mountain, he has used the eyes of a man to see her suffering, thinking all the while that he was the only one who knew, and that she was the one who was blind to the torture on her body and her soul. "Let's sign a treaty," she says. Her voice is tender with warmth and a soft caress.

"A treaty on what?" he asks, knowing the answer long before she has the chance to speak.

"On what we've become. On your love."

"And yours."

And there, forever etched on the window of the worn-out, old cafe, the shadows of the two destitute souls tangle together in the dying light of a fairy tale ending.

Last Night, I Dreamed of Whales

Last Night, I Dreamed of Whales

I wake up in a lush field of greens, thinking it is real.

Isn't that what life after death is supposed to feel like? You never realize that your limited time on Earth is over, so you keep on mistaking between the real and the purgatory you are handed. The rights to refuse or accept never belong to you, so you trudge on the path to salvation, grudgingly, hoping that somehow, with the crumbs of virtues you had built when you were alive, God will take a second look at your poor, pathetic case.

And his translucent soul hangs in front of me on the weeping willows, telling me that this is yet another I can't escape. I wonder if he holds a grudge against me since that time I told him to either die or fuck off because I couldn't go on listening to his moody, absurd musing on what it meant to love. Well, he ended up dying. And I can't say I'm better or worse. A car accident and a long coma––that's better. Forever stuck here with his long ramble of gibberish because I can't understand dead people's language––that's worse.

As usual, our old (and long passed away) tabby cat, Becky,

leads me and the ghost of my lover to the dark shade of a cherry blossom tree. The petals are flying in the air, twirling and whirling in circles. A few petals fall on Becky's soft, hairy head. She shakes them off with annoyance and sneezes. Judging from the passing of winter to spring, I must have been dreaming for a long time. The scale tips from a long coma to an eternity season in this beautiful purgatory.

"I've always been allergic to flowers," Becky says.

"It's strange. I thought only people were capable of being allergic to flowers," I reply, picking petals from her silky fur, sneaking a few pets on her soft forehead. She purrs.

"Then it's your fault for stereotyping humans and stereotyping cats," she grumbles, leaning into my touch. *Yes*, I think, *as if anyone would believe a cat's word.*

"Alright. My fault. Dear lady, can you stop being so sassy?"

"Can't help it. It comes with me as a full-package deal."

His ghost holds my hand in his cold palm, shakes it lightly to make me focus on him. He places a finger on his lips, *Hush*, he seems to say, then laughs like a child, the usual laugh that rings in my ears like the cathedral's silver bells singing every evening.

I remember when he was still alive. The evenings in our high-rise condo, watching a thousand sunsets as the watercolor purple cascaded over the sky like Monet's water lily portrait. "Sadness," he said, "can only be this beautiful." We would sit on our tiny apartment's balcony, guessing which cathedral's bells were tolling for the poor, unfortunate souls, forever suffering on Earth just to find a way to salvation––something their money can't purchase but that gives a good illusion of similarity. "It's the one in the West," he would always say, and I would laugh at his childlike enthusiasm with every little game we

140

played. I knew it was my turn to counter him. No matter which direction I pointed to, or whether there was actually a cathedral in that direction or not, he wouldn't care.

All we wanted to do at that time was make small arguments, talking about whatever came to our minds. Speaking in tongues just to hear the other person's voice. The world was too large and we were the only two living souls in it.

But the arguments grew out of reach. And later on, they were no longer arguments. They became the ugly throwing of dishes, loud crashes of TV sets, curses, and words we would later regret ever uttering. Like, "I wish we had never met." Like, "I'd rather not love you."

Like him cursing me lovingly, "I hope you die a terrible death."

And I retorted grudgingly, "Go fucking die or get the fuck out of here, you stupid motherfucker. I'm too tired of your shit."

It's strange, I often wondered then, how we were surrounded by all these cathedrals, Christ and whatnot, and yet we couldn't find peace. Either the peace within or the peace without, we couldn't find any at all. I still wonder about it now. But his laughter is distracting, and the moment the sound of his laughter reaches my ears, all scores are settled. I squeeze his cold palms and let it go at that.

"You seem to be quite easy to appease, as always," Becky says as she sneezes and vigorously shakes her fluffy head to get rid of the cherry blossom petals.

I turn around. The mist of pastel pink flowers is everywhere, with a dash of the sad strings of wisteria and the calming lavender bushes. On the trail ahead, there's nothing but a carpet of bluebells and evergreen trees. The sense of hope is palpitating in the air. I only need to breathe to feel the source of life coursing through my veins. Superficially, of course, because my body is just the construct of what I remember, and my soul is teetering between the world of the living and the dead.

"Yes, I am very easy to appease." I smile.

There are places that make you want to leave. There are places that make you want to stay buried inside. I wonder if the choice is ever up to us.

He squats down beside Becky and brushes the petals off her round head. She returns the favor with a loud, unladylike purr, eyes closing, completely indulging herself in the unconditional love that he is bestowing on her. I shrug; he's always been her favorite human, alive or dead.

The soft morning light shines on his black hair. The strands reflect back a gentle color of platinum gold. His face lights up with a gentle smile. His eyes are black as black can be—the color of the nights where it was so dark that the drunken man couldn't help but get lost on the familiar routes. His bony fingers lovingly scratch Becky's head and cheeks; the soft tips quickly appear and disappear in the black spot on the cat's fur.

"Becky, you know what, you make me want to be a cat," I say, dropping myself down next to him and ruffling the cat's head in a ridiculous fit of jealousy.

"It's not me who makes you want to be a cat," she mocks, licking her paws, "It's him."

I turn to look at him. His eyes watch me with the same tenderness and love, before the greatest war killed the passion within us and the black dog ate him up inside. Before all things led back to Milton's *Paradise Lost*. Before we became human.

"It's alright," he says, "All is forgiven and forgotten."

And I smile back, hopeless in my futile attempt to hold onto hope, because what else do I have left but that heartless monster?

"Man, you are a lost cause," Becky snickers, which distorts her normally lethargic cat face into something wicked. Like a human. But Becky can't be wicked, I know, because she's been through enough to know better than exerting her energy unnecessarily on something that won't bring her any food. I push Becky aside and lay my head on his lap, trying to relive sad memories that were gone a long time ago.

"Do you know the story about the whales, Becky?"

"Yeah, you're gonna talk about that after pushing this lady aside?"

"The story goes something like this," I say, ignoring her sarcastic remark.

"Do you know the story about the whales?" He asked me one night as we lay our bare skin on the soft mattress, getting ready to sleep.

"What about the whales?" I turned to face him. He always had this addictive sadness on his face—these gentle eyes, these pale pink lips, which turned soft and darkish red whenever he bit them—that get me to jump down into the abyss of the faintest faith.

Truth was, I don't really care much for the whales and their story. But he looked at me with his eyes full of sorrow, and what else could I do but ask him about them?

"Last night, I dreamed of them."

"Another weird dream of yours?"

"Don't say that," he commanded, his eyes squinting in disapproval. "You know I hate it when you say that."

Of course I wanted to say that. I wanted to say that every time, just to see his frown, the curve of his lovely pout, and the long lashes when he squinted his eyes. And I would always stop right at the

143

moment he dropped the command.

"You're right, Becky. I'm a lost cause," I laugh as I tweak a strand of his hair and tuck it behind his ear. The memory is breaking and falling apart as his lush hair slips through my fingers, only to descend, featherlight, on his forehead and everywhere. Each time I pick up a strand, he returns the favor with a gentle smile.

"I—"

"I want to kiss you."

"You don't want to hear about the whales?" He frowned again. I knew that with one wrong choice, there would be a high chance that I would have to sleep alone. And no living being would like that.

"Kiss me then. Give me a kiss and I will hear your whale stories."

"I'll sleep in the guest room then." He got up.

"I want to kiss you." The words come out of my mouth before my brain can register what is going on.

What is in the past has found its way to linger here in the present. What is in the present tries to find its way to hold onto the future. The word is in the going, and it is going fast. I am lost in the maze of my own creation, until he finds me. With a slight motion, he bends down and ever so lightly, gives me a peck on my lips. They are cold and wet, and they are nothing like the pout he had bestowed on me when we were on that balcony, surrounded by cathedrals and poverty.

"Wait, I want to hear that story. Really, I want to hear it. Tell me your whale story."

I put my arms around his tiny waist and pushed him down. I always marveled at how he was so willing to let me take command, despite knowing who was in charge of our relationship.

"What now?" he said, feigning annoyance; but his eyes said, "Fine, you're allowed to kiss me."

"Tell me about the whales." I leaned in. His warm breath touched my thin lips. Some of the dead skin on my lips got in the way, but it was quickly cast aside as we drowned in the ecstasy of a lifelong kiss.

"He dreamed of whales," I say, my hands reaching out to catch the petal flowers falling from his hair.

"Yeah, the whales who turn into humans," Becky mumbles in her half-asleep state.

"Yes." I stop to swallow the bile that is rising in my throat. "About the whales who turn into humans."

In that whale story, there was a prince who always went to the seashore, watching the whales dancing in the ocean. He fell in love with the tiniest whale among the herd, but he couldn't swim out there. He prayed to the moon goddess to turn him into a whale. The moon goddess said, "What is done can't be undone," and turned his wish into reality.

As the prince, now being a whale, swam out to the distant ocean, the tiniest whale was nowhere to be found. Unbeknownst to him, the tiniest whale had fallen in love with him when he was still a little boy. And unbeknownst to him, under the full moon when she turned 16, she prayed to the moon goddess to turn her into a human. The moon goddess said, "What is done can't be undone."

And the moment the whale could walk on the seashore was also the moment the prince reached the bottom of the ocean. Standing on the sliding sand, the girl stared at the prince-whale on the distant horizon. Forever and ever, the prince could never step on the shore. Forever and ever, the girl couldn't swim back to the ocean.

"Why are your dreams always so sad?" I said, holding his head closer to my chest and resting my chin on his dark felt carpet of hair.

I don't know what I wanted to achieve then. Perhaps I wanted to console him. Perhaps I wanted to go another round with him.

Or perhaps at that moment, when we were on the verge of being fully awake and nearly sleeping, I only wanted the moon goddess to let us be human, err on the side of being too human, if she could.

"Because sometimes, it is what it is. What is done cannot be undone."

"Are you crying again? How many times have you cried since the start of this dream already?" Becky comes over and as a way of fluffy consolation, she steps on my chest and lies across my throat, purring.

"Becky, I can't breathe." I sniffle.

"Should I step down then?"

"No, stay right where you are," I say, feeling his now stone-cold hand cover my tear-filled eyes, "It's not your fault. It's never your fault."

"Then whose fault is it?"

"The whales," I say, holding his bony hand in mine, gently stroking each tender finger and feeling their non-existence, "and the fucking moon goddess."

Because didn't the moon goddess say, in her high indifference of omniscient power, "What is done cannot be undone?"

I fall asleep to the sound of his laughter and Becky's purr, knowing full well that the moment I wake up, it will be yet another dream.

And when I dream, it will get me back to how things used to be. The beauty in the garbage dump of what we believed we could get through if we put in just a little more effort--leave the arguments open-ended so we can come back later with bitter resentments until the hate festers into grudges we can't outrun or outwit. Am I the one at fault, or is he? Eventually, the answer doesn't amount to anything more than a new topic for the next battle. We live on ugly truth, thinking it is sweet sugar, convincing ourselves that the longer we hold on, the more decadent the taste.

But it never gets to the 'decadence' part, does it? I mean, who'd die from cancer?

"Basically, everyone." Becky rolls her eyes so hard I can hear them turn in their sockets.

"But he was recovering."

"Then he relapsed."

"He recovered from that, too."

"Another relapse."

"How many does it make when he reaches the end of the tragedy?" I scoff, my fingers playing with his vanishing lower half. "Two? Three?"

"About that many."

"Fuck relapse. Fuck cancer. Fuck death. Fuck everything that dares to think it can live happily ever after. Fuck the moon goddess—especially her."

"Whatever. You're just regretting cursing him when he was too much of a burden for you to carry." Becky yawns, curls up on my chest. I feel her comforting weight on my body, as if all of this were real, and he was there, and Becky didn't die from a heart attack. Someone once warned me to be careful of memory because it will bring me nothing but misery. I asked them why, because the past was so beautiful it was hard to believe the things I remembered would come back to hurt me. And that person said the reason was exactly that: beautiful things that were no longer here; they were either perished or destroyed by our own hands. Sure, the memory was lovely, but the present will always return, and a thousand reminiscences won't change the fact that the show must go on. Living like that, having to jumping between what you once had and no longer have, will never have again, they said, isn't it a form of purgatory on Earth? Their smile was painted with nothing but pure, unadulterated sorrow.

"Becky, death is a heavy thing to carry on your shoulders. I carry mine already; how can I fucking carry his on top of that boulder?" I snicker, choking with an ocean of thoughts.

Becky turns silent. Maybe she falls asleep; a cat never bothers too much with anything or anyone that is irrelevant to her immediate needs and pleasure. Or maybe she knows how excruciating the toll of death is on the people left behind after a life goes out. I glance at his soul, hovering over the blossoms; his face remains serene, as if it was just yesterday when we first met and I told him he was the one I'd never stop searching for. "It's cruel, isn't it? To know that the end is inevitable, and it will always take a bad turn, but you still choose to walk on the path anyways," I say to no one at all. Becky wouldn't understand, and he wouldn't answer with words, just a rueful smile and a subdued nod.

"See, I never meant half of the things I said. And most of the time, I throw out insults because they ease the frustration in my mind. When I told you, 'Go to hell,' I meant, 'Why is it so hard to have a normal life?' Same with 'Either fucking die to get out.' What I wanted to say was—if God had been more benevolent toward us, He would take me instead of you."

My breath hitches. I don't know what the use of all these sentimentalities is, but a nagging voice in my head keeps urging me to go on, because this is the last chance. Of what? I don't even know.

"You know, I watched you die every day. The hair falling

out, the sunken cheeks, the thinning figure, and through it all, I kept cursing, pleading, begging on my knees, 'Please, please, please take him away quickly.' How much can I suffer? The answer is two years, three months, fifteen days, and a bit over three hours." I laugh, coughing to hide the hurt that is growing in my voice. "The truth is, I have always loved you. But saying that now won't change anything, right? What is done can't be undone."

I watch him in great apprehension. What will he do? Will he reply, at least? Will he throw a tantrum like he used to do when he was alive? Will he say it's alright, that his pain wasn't my fault, that I was allowed to feel hurt, too, that we are humans, and I have the same freedom to suffer as he does?

But none of those scenes happens. Becky's voice grows harsh and masculine, with an extremely low tone, almost graveling: "Sir, can you hear me? If you can, please grip my fingers as a reply."

A rough, cylindrical object is shoved inside my palm. I look at it, thinking it is a wooden stick. To my horror, that object turns out to be a man's finger, sterile and dried with the pungent scent of ether and sanitizer. Becky keeps saying, "Can you hear me, sir?" And I keep shaking my head, No, no, no. My eyes search for his figure, but the world of dreams is shattering to nothingness. I scream his name as despair is seeping through my skin like Heracles's Hydra poison. "Please," I beg, "One more dream with him is all I'm asking for." But God has other plans. He doesn't discriminate when categorizing the living and the dead. I wake up to the sound of my vital signs being measured by the cranky machines. Becky's voice, which I heard, is the voice of the old doctor in charge of my resuscitation. "Sir," he repeats, "can you hear me?"

I blink as a way of answering. My whole body is paralyzed, and the pain is rushing through each inch of my flesh.

"You were in a car accident. Based on your lab results, besides the broken bones and the bruising, you have nothing to worry about," the doctor assures me in his good humor. "To be alive after a hit like that––it's almost like you're protected by God."

I stare at him, eyes wide with unspeakable agony and self-mockery. The words he said are like daggers aiming straight at my ruined heart. "Protected by God"––I never prayed for another rent on this Earth. Clenching my hands with difficulty, I feel the rough texture of something––paper? Is it a card? Who's it from? I try to lift my left arm where the object is lodged in my palm, but the pain is more of a beast than I had imagined, and I can't conquer it with willpower alone. Grunting, I call the doctor, my lips bleeding to enhance the already terrifying scene. "Paper. Left hand."

"Oh? Right. You were grasping onto the photo so tightly I couldn't pry it out. Let me see––here's yours."

He places the photo before me. It is a Polaroid of him and Becky sleeping on our white, velvety upholstered sofa in the soft light of the living room. He had just got back from his chemo. Becky was getting thinner due to old age and her heart problem. They sat for the photo, him smiling sweetly, and Becky curling on his lap, striking her most beautiful pose. The two were forever trapped in that tiny frame of the photograph. I cry, reading the note he scribbled messily at the bottom: "The truth is, I have always loved you."

The Lord gave, and the Lord hath taken away; blessed be the name of the Lord.
– Job 1:21

The Pale Blue Queen

"You look better than the last time I saw you," she says. "Your dark circles seems to be improving."

And here I sit, in the chair that is all too familiar to me. I sometimes wonder if the chair would hate having someone sitting on it constantly. I wonder if it hates me.

The cushion is almost threadbare; the red color has faded with the arduous passage of time. Perhaps when it was young, and life was still easy with its slow rhythm, the cushion had been a beautiful gypsy decor. Well, not anymore. And no one's bothered enough to change it. Certainly not the café's owner.

"I'm not bothered enough to notice it. That's all."

"But surely you're bothered enough to sleep early." She smiles, and with that, all the memory we share iscoming back to remind me of the distance between us. And I just hate hate hate how the smile never conveys her true feelings.

"How's it going?" I ask. It's more a rhetorical question than a signal of personal concern. Because I know full well what her answer will be.

"It's going good, really. How about you?"

Yes, it's always "going good." I stare at her unmoving eyes. She always fixated those pale blue eyes on my face. The pale blue eyes that refuse the temptation to profess any sentimentality other than "it's going good," to open up the door, to reveal a part of her soul that is deeper than just the surface level.

I smirk. The whole fiasco makes me sick.

"What are you staring at?" she asks, giggling. Even her giggling at my dumbstruck face is a rhetorical act, which is all too familiar to her and too strange for me.

"Nothing."

"Come on. You just keep on staring." She tugs at my shirt sleeve.

Yes, my darling, I keep on staring. Because where else can I look when the meaning of my existence is right there in front of me? But those words are forbidden, and I let love simmer until it becomes an active volcano, ready to crack the earth open.

"When's he coming? Isn't it past the meeting time already?" I say, breaking the glass wall between us.

She withdraws her hand and pulls both of them back to a safe distance. The same distance we dare not cross: a hand's length and an ocean apart. I keep swimming in that unfathomable ocean. I never succeed in finding the right shore, and I'm always drowning drowning drowning in those pale blue eyes.

"He says he'll be a little late," she replies timidly. An awkward silence comes, spreading out like a deadly disease. I wonder when this disease began affecting me. The silence dissects my flesh, cuts my bones, and burns my nerves to ashes.

"Hey, how about we stop this whole shitty, gaudy theatrical act?" I blurt out, quicker than my brain can comprehend the consequence.

"Stopping what?"

"Stopping this," I touch her hand slightly, closing the hand's-length distance between us. Yet, the ocean distance is still there. As I expected, she inches her hands away. Each inch produces an unbearable tug on my heart string.

I laugh derisively at my pathetic self. *Why are you killing me this slowly, darling? Do have some mercy on me and kill me in a swift blow of separation. You can gouge out my heart, sever my head, and in that triumphant death, I will keep on loving you the same. Longingly, tenderly, ardently.*

"You didn't have to come if you didn't want to," she says. Her words bring me back to the café's noisy reality.

"No, I didn't mean that. I just said it without thinking," I reply, trying to create the same smile she uses on me. Then, realizing the embarrassing failure as I see the growing pity in her eyes, I quickly shut up.

"Why don't we just leave?"

"Why don't you stay for a little while?"

"He won't come."

"Then why bother coming here at all?"

"Does it matter? Do you want me to stay? Or do you want me to leave? Would his coming here be more comforting to you? Or would it not?"

She bursts out all of these rhetorical questions. The questions I try to hide behind my disgusting gentleness. The questions I try to erase from our conversation whenever we have the chance to meet. The questions that hurt. The questions that wound us everywhere between the what-could-have-been and the what-will-never-be.

"I bother," I tell her, "I bother enough to come here, to listen to your silly talk about all your ex-boyfriends, your current boyfriends, and your future boyfriends. But..."

"But what?"

Yes, but what? I think about future; there are endless opportunities, lying before me like luxury gifts behind a glass display window at Christmas. I could buy it if I have enough in me -- money, courage, the will to take what's rightfully mine despite the thunder and fury of any higher being. Then I think about her clenched hands whenever she sits opposite me, talking. Her boyfriend sits on the left side of the table; she sits on the right side, facing me. The conversation is always boring. *Oh, you're working in that field. No, I'm not knowledgeable about it. Really, you read those kinds of books? Working out is great. Yes, I can see the results on your body.*

But what? I ask myself. But I am not bothered enough to take your invitation, to just pack things up and run away, to be free. I know that freedom might not act on the promises that it is giving us with sweet, honeycomb poison. Yet, there's the hope, and there's me and you, trying to fill the ocean with buckets of sand, until we realize that it will never be enough, and we should replace the "but" with the "what if." Darling, what if we can fly?

"Let's leave, then," I say, withdrawing my hand from hers. "Let's continue the conversation at another time."

"I'll bring a better person next time, I promise."

"Don't." I fix my eyes on hers, engraving every little detail of her face on my brain. "Don't make the ocean bigger than it already is." Rubbing my brows, I bow to her, accepting my defeat. The more loving one is always me. The winner will always be her. Smiling bitterly, I speak the truth of my heart, "After all, I'm not bothered enough to care about the men in your life." I feel my throat burning with every word. They are making a revolution, and my rationality—my cowardice—is losing hold of the strongest forte.

"Don't bring them," I repeat. "It's you that I care about."

There goes my little declaration of independence. And the enemy—the pale blue queen—sits there on her throne, knowing my every move, and smiles. Taken aback by the smile that resembles the blooming flowers of the first spring after the long, solitary winter, I accept my defeat.

"Let's give this a try, then," she says.

"Give what a try?"

"This whole thing," she giggles. "This you and me." She inches her hands forward. Her fingers wrap around mine, closing whatever oceans and mountains there were between us. "Let's give love a try."

Museum of Echoes

The girl puts the thick book back on the shelf. The yellow pages are heavy with words and the burden of the time it has lived through. She jots down the name, the title, the opinions—or rather, the thoughts that everyone before her had conjured up—and she is now simply echoing back onto her blank notebook. Hemingway. *A Farewell to Arms*. Machismo prose style. Like shooting at point-blank range.

She flips the page. Another name appears. Faulkner. Between grief and nothing, etc. A soft thud rings in the empty museum; the sound reverberates off the rotting bookshelves like a wake-up call for those who are walking without eyes and reading without ears. She jerks up her head. The grandfather clock at the end of the hallway points at half-past six. She still has time for another book. Another voice. Another echo from the past. With palpitating breath and fervent ambition, she reaches for one more book on the shelf. The name quickly catalogues itself into the system. Albert Camus. *The First Man*. Absurdism.

No one knows where she comes from, but they all know why she is there at the Museum of Echoes, the tall, grey building that was rumored to store the first draft of all the greatest books. The names behind them are long dead. The knowledge between the pages has become so sacred that nobody bothers to understand; they'd rather revere it like an ikon for their blissful ignorance. So a rich philanthropist—as the case always is— builds the gaudy building in a shape that would make Howard Roark kill himself over and over again to store what he terms "nothing but echoes."

Because no one understands the first word when it appears on Hemingway's typewritten page, or Kafka's handwritten letter. Or perhaps the philanthropist simply thinks it is a mystery, how the voice of the past reaches the action of the future, but no real culprit is there to take responsibility for it. *The Catcher in the Rye* and the assassinations. The philanthropist thinks he is a wise man.

But the misfortune unfolds not long after. Many writers begin to flood the gate of the Museum of Echoes. Some come by to find their voice. Others come to look for a higher meaning, the cause to keep on writing, the reason to be, and on the rare occasion, the reason not to be. A few, like her, come to the museum, hoping to place their names among the shelves. She has done her research, far too much of it. The Lost Generation. The Beat Generation. And she is ready to be the next Gertrude, hosting her own salon, becoming the giant of her time. After all, why can't she? Literary awards she has won, yes, though they are not renowned, but she has every right to be proud. And she has every right to belong here. Much like the philanthropist, people like her think they can become the echo.

Then where is the misfortune? A stranger might ask. And the seasoned city people, who are so used to the curious stares, the gossip, the journalists flocking to their houses, asking questions, investigating the sudden disappearance overnight of some Mr. A or Ms. B, would just shake their heads. The first rule about the Museum of Echoes is that a person is not allowed to discuss matters involving the Museum of Echoes. The closest thing to an answer a tourist to this city can get is an old piece of newspaper on the bulletin board outside the central bus station. The front page is darkened with age, but the headline is stark against the white board:

DANGER: 15 MYSTERIOUS MISSING PEOPLE LAST SEEN INSIDE THE MUSEUM OF ECHOES

Those 15 people were not the first, and sadly, 10 years since then, they are not the last. Mysteries only attract more writers, authors, the named and the unnamed alike. It is easy to see the reason why: the innate desire to be the chosen one is in human nature. Everyone has their own race. While ordinary people are racing to buy the best meat at the cheapest price and cry over luxurious eggs born from caged hens (advertised as free-range, of course), writers are struggling to win another race. Whose name will be the last one to outlive the rest of humanity? In the quick chase to get to the throne, perhaps they forget not everyone can become a saint. And even saints are forgotten.

Life has its own way of going on. In due course, the journalists get bored of the matter. The city raises caution. The ordinary people return to their way of living. More meat. More I-can't-believe-it's-not-butter. Fewer eggs. The philanthropist builds a few more museums and university halls. His name is engraved therein. And the writers? No one ever notices their disappearance.

The first mistake she makes, then, is to think that she is different.

Or rather, she trusts in the one thing that God has given

humanity in jest: intelligence. She uses a coil of thread, tying one line around her ankle, and places the coil at the gate of the museum. Based on her primeval thought, or what Greek history has taught women like her, Ariadne's thread will lead the way to salvation. In the vainglorious moment of revering her own ingenious idea, taken from a book she read a few years back, she seems to forget one crucial role of the thread: Ariadne was running away from her tormentor. She is heading straight toward the beast, waiting in its chamber to devour her whole. As for the character in the book she read, who knew where he ended up? Blank page after blank page, isn't the reader the one deciding a book's ending? And so it seems, to the seasoned city people who chance upon her entrance to the Museum of Echoes, her ending is also a foregone conclusion.

A thud in the disquietude of the night. She turns a page under her phone's flashlight. Jean-Paul Sartre. *Being and Nothingness.* Faulkner said, "Between grief and nothing…" She starts drafting her own story. A vagabond on the road, begging for alms, finding meanings to life, then he stumbles on—what? She scratches her head. She flips the pages. A name pops out. José Saramago. *Blindness.* He stumbles upon a strange disease. She writes down the first line of her soon-to-be prize-winning. A no-brainer, if she might say so. It all comes to her so naturally that sometimes she is amazed by her own—what do normal people call it again? Right, talent. Black ink appears on white paper, thin and transparent like a cheap carbon copy running out of ink:

He was but a vagabond on the road searching for a place to belong. His baggage was heavy before, but now he has none. No place to call home, and no one to share the last remnants of his life with. As he stood there underneath the roof of a strange house in the otherwise perfectly aligned buildings and condominiums, a dizziness shot through his brain like a bazooka rocket. The next moment he opened his eyes, he realized he was blind...

She bites the tip of the gel pen. The ink is bleeding everywhere and nowhere in between, but it doesn't quite ring out. The sound doesn't reach the mass. The voice is hollow. The story doesn't differ from a thousand other stories in the Museum of Echoes. She throws the notebook away, heaves a sigh, wondering, *Is this all there is?* She wants the heart-racing plot, the unique style that ten years later someone will label after her name, the fame—yes, but more than that—the mark on this earth proving that she is here. She had come to this museum with so much hope, a hope that no ordinary human living an ordinary life, worrying about egg prices, would understand: the hope to be.

And yet, the deeper she traverses into the labyrinths of this museum, the more she realizes the stark, lonely truth: there is no road on this earth that is untraveled. If the world could tell its story of death and rebirth, the giants on these shelves have already finished relaying its pathos. She is, as the seasoned city people have rightly assumed, another stranger. Missing person? Perhaps. She still has a way out. Ariadne's thread is still hanging loosely on her ankle—the sweet temptation of life, the last salvation of sanity. But the story is unfinished.

So she picks up the notebook and rewrites the opening. She has gotten stuck there for a while. No opening line seems to befit her grandiose storyline. No ending would justify it either. It should shake the world as she knows it. It should make everyone reading the first syllable tremble in fear. Look at her, the first woman who can write with such vengeance and reverence that no other woman writer will ever compete.

She imagines herself standing on the podium, giving the prize-winning lecture, inducted into the Writers' Hall of Fame. Doris Lessing. *Prisons We Choose to Live Inside.* The prize is but a lottery game. She can't let it deter her from her goal. The protagonist is blind. The road he leads his stray cattle on to salvation will be an arduous one, but it will ring true. It will be hers alone. With that determination shining brightly in her mind like a half-mad Ophelia, she goes deeper into the Museum of Echoes. The coil extends itself a bit further.

Outside, darkness begins to cast its shroud. The weather man forecasts an upcoming storm. The people on the street hurry home after a long day at work. They nail their doors and windows shut. The city warns of a three-day closure. All transportation services will stop after 10 p.m. that day. Public places—including libraries, parks, and museums—will be temporarily closed. Listening to the broadcast news, the old, conscientious guard locks the heavy, ornamental gates of the Museum of Echoes. His brows furrow, wondering if there are still people inside it. His aging eyes miss the sight of the coil of Ariadne's thread the writer placed at the door a few days prior. He goes home, safe and secure with the knowledge that there is shelter waiting for him. The steel doors click shut, cutting the thread. The coil falls down the stone steps of the museum's porch.

Life has a way of going on. In the eye of the upcoming storm, no one remembers the existence of the soon-to-be missing person, the soon-to-be prize-winning woman writer in the dark hallway, buried between the bookshelves of dead names and undying flames.

Deep in the dusty basement, the writer barely hears anything about the storm. The voice from the loudspeaker in the

161

upper corner of the marble pillar has long been shut off. The electricity is gradually losing the battle against the viciousness of thunder and lightning. Meanwhile, she is too busy reading a classic by James Joyce. *Ulysses*. Mr. Bloom and the much-discussed scene of the court. She flips through the pages; the words slide through her brain like water seeping through a sieve. Nothing is retained as her own. She keeps remembering her professor's dissection of the paragraph. A thought sparks up: Isn't this about James Joyce's personal experience? She jots down the words, "internalization of thoughts and fears, stream-of-consciousness prose style, maybe first of its kind, interruption of reality to represent the multi-faceted grotesque facts and realistic lives of all characters involved," and so on. None of this is her opinion. It is easily traced to familiar sources in literary journals and essays from her alma mater. It would be unfair to say that she hasn't read *Ulysses*: she has read it cover to cover, ten times or so. But like catching a fish with bare hands, the meaning keeps escaping her. Perhaps it has a life of its own, and that life has no place for a great writer such as herself. She can't write a Leopold Bloom or a Stephen Dedalus, but she will write someone far greater, far more memorable, far more everything, all at once.

She will write someone like this vagabond with his strange, sudden blindness.

The thunder strikes. The ceiling lighting shouts a loud shriek and the museum retreats to its rightful place: the enshrouding, moldy mantle of nothingness. The writer looks up in fright; from her vantage point, the bookshelf and the echoes of Hemingway, Kafka, Joyce, Faulkner, and their contemporaries, or the ones before them, are no longer giants. They are a monstrous existence, waiting for her to step right into their mouths, teeth so sharp they will tear her flesh apart, tongues so prickly with thorns that they will break her bones. They are looming all around her in the chamber, waiting with a palpitating silence—so pregnant with life one can listen to its heavy breathing—for her to fall. She turns on the flashlight. The hallway stretches out to an eternity of human history. She is the only living person inside the realm of the dead. The echoes can't reach through the storm outside. Her cry for help is long overdue. No one is coming to salvage the lost soul of yet another delusion.

An echo rings in the dark. In trembling, she turns her head toward the eerie sound of the past. It says, *Whatever you are looking for, it is not in here.* Tongue tied, lips sealed, she picks up the notebook, and against her better judgment, she walks toward the echo, traveling deeper into the hallway of the undisturbed slumber. The sky shakes with anger. She halts in her tracks, listening to the sound of heaven's ridicule, bearing the gods' jeering at her futile and pathetic attempt of trying to recreate a Tower of Babel. Yet, she persists. Only she alone can prove how right—or how wrong—she can be, and she won't let a deity who reigns without existing dictate the life she lives. A book falls off the shelf and lands at her feet. Søren Kierkegaard. *Fear and Trembling.* "Faith begins precisely where thinking leaves off." Did she or did she not answer the immortal question for every writer—the ones before her and the ones after her? To be great is to not think at all but just act on it.

But what is "it?" The muse? The scorching desire to tell a story? The cause for her fervent passion to put her pen on the blank page? What is behind all this fiasco that people call writing? Why hasn't she been able to write something greater than *Absalom, Absalom? For Whom the Bell Tolls? One Hundred Years of Solitude?* Why can't she create something more grandiose than a vagabond standing under the roof of a strange house's porch, waiting for life to happen, only to stumble upon a sudden blindness, coming out of nowhere?

She browses the shelves farther at the back. The hallways seem to stretch to an eternity of time and space. Mario Vargas Llosa. *The War of the End of the World.* She hasn't read this one yet, but the title promises a new source of ideas. Her fingers turn the yellow pages swiftly; her eyes scan the words like they are nothing but a valuable commodity. Some phrases are stored; some are quickly discarded as irrelevant. No one wants to read a page without a memorable quote. A picture-perfect sentence in a flower frame, applicable to everyone and anyone, but that influences no one at the same time, something that is empty of meaning but can gather a few minutes of fame. She ponders. Is that what she is looking for? "Death isn't enough. It doesn't remove the stain." She startles and drops the book onto the carpeted floor. In a surge of mounting fear, she looks around. Where is she? Why has she come here after all? The purpose—what is her original purpose? Her vagabond... She looks at the notebook. In front of her eyes, the story unfolds its next chapter. But the writing isn't hers. The setting, the tone, the philosophical undertone—all of it—it is literary greatness on loan, with great interest and a tight deadline. She reads the sentences, her eyes wide with greed:

"The vagabond flounders in the rain. Though his sight is stolen from him, he knows it is for a grander scheme that the Lord has planned. Many a mortal man has traversed his path, but none of them receives this gift, disguised as a punishment. He knows, then, that he is the chosen one. To live is to suffer. To suffer is to understand the beauty in living to the fullest. To understand the beauty of it all, then, is to immerse himself in the greatest humiliation, the gravest misery. The vagabond understands why God has called out, "Suffer little children to come unto me." Only the suffering children see the benevolence and the mercy of God. The creators of this world built a hell so that the suffering children can see how beautiful paradise is. And that paradise will forever be lost to whoever has perfect sight to see. It is not the eyes, nay—the vagabond mulls over his thoughts as he trembles in the rabbit hole, the rainwater rising to his knees—it is the spirit that feels and becomes. So, suffering I am and suffering I will be, until darkness devours me and delivers me to Him who bore me..."

The writer flips the page over, but the paragraph ends there. She shuffles the pages in frustration. Where is the rest of the story? Where will the vagabond end? How come he is facing such a heavy theological dilemma, one she cannot think of on her own, leaving the readers hanging in temptation, waiting for more, counting his steps, his breath, his every move? She crumples the page; an unknown shame and anger begin to surface. She wants to claim that it is she who writes these excellent phrases; every line is a fantastic option for a social media flaunt. But deep inside her conscious mind, she knows it is not. The sheer talent of composing such thoughts, the deep understanding of psychological analysis and Christian damnation, the combination of Søren Kierkegaard, Friedrich Nietzsche, and Jean-Paul Sartre and merge the knowledge into something more magnificent than her existence could ever be. There was no writer before with such glorious prose and there will be no one writing with such beauty after the story is finished. No, it is not her who weaves this dream within a dream. Something whispers in her mind, and she is paralyzed with a terror never before known in her life as a writer. The trepidation seeps through her pores and drops to the page in beads of sweat, wetting the punctuations and the phrase, "So, suffering I am and suffering I will be, until darkness devours me and delivers me to Him who bore me..."

She knows who the author is. It is the echo.

With unsteady feet, she wanders deeper into the museum, unaware that her Ariadne's thread is trailing behind her, the cord already cut. Her fingers run through the binding of each book. "Sophia descended from the thirteenth aeon..." No, this is not quite the effect she wants. "The dead can survive as part of the lives of those that still live..." Almost, yes, but not the right words. "Freeing yourself was one thing, claiming ownership of that freed self was another." Yes, yes, yes. In the ascension of madness, she claws at the books, shoving them down the shelves, swallowing each phrase, each word, each punctuation mark like it is her lifeline. The way out is through. She scribbles in her notebook; the writing becomes erratic and unhinged. She needs the story of the vagabond to continue. She needs him to be different. She needs a climax with the power to shake the earth, cause a rumble amongst the highest academic circles. She wants to be the canon amongst the canons. She hungers for fame, for the eternal remembrance, for reverence long overdue because people have been blinded to her sheer talent. The books trail after her lunatic footsteps; their laughter rings in the dark, pregnant with ridicule and contempt. A mere human dares to disturb the holiness of the giants' sorrow—nay, she is worse: she dares to dream.

Outside, the storm has continued its rage for two days.

The seasoned city people glance through their curtained

windows and heave a weary sigh. They know the gods are angry, though they have no knowledge of why. Someone is reaching for the height of vanity—of that, they are sure. But ordinary people such as themselves, whose most valued possession is a job—and for some, a well-taken-care-of home and garden—vanity is outside of their reach. They remember a monk once said when passing by their city, "Nothing is vanity; having everything is also vanity." They didn't understand his meaning then. But seeing his eyes as he watched the construction of the Museum of Echoes, the rueful wisdom bowing to the willful ignorance of the filthy rich, they can feel his sorrow just enough to turn their heads away and cower in shame.

Long after the monk left, the seasoned city people tried their best to forget about the museum. It is an eyesore, a testament to their stupidity and their cowardice in the face of immense wealth and the allure of money. They swear in church every Sunday morning to their suffering Lord on high that they do not—will never—succumb to greed. But the Lord knoweth and the Lord will testify for them how tempting the taste of dry, aged, medium-rare steak in a Michelin-star-rated restaurant feels on the tongue. Between being and nothingness, perhaps only Jean-Paul Sartre is brave enough to choose the latter. After all, Jean-Paul Sartre has become an ideal, while they are still living. The first and foremost condition of being is the will to do anything to survive.

It is safe to say, then, that the seasoned city people slowly forget about the monk and their cowardice.

On the other hand, there is a new class of human, a wave of country bumpkins immigrating to the city from the borderline of their poverty. They flood through the gate with the money from the sales of their land and their houses. Millions of dollars raining down without an ounce of effort, or, as the philosophers call them, the nouveau riche. The seasoned city people coin another term for them: the brainless blind. Holding tightly to their empty savings accounts, they look down on the blessed ignorance of the newly immigrated people with a deep-seated hatred. Jealousy. No, not quite. It is rooted deeper than that. Like a cycle, the old hates the new; the poor ridicule the rich; the working class abhor the petite bourgeoise; the slaves loathe the burden of the ruling class. Through thousands of years, the seeds have firmly planted themselves in the fabric of history. How can the simple minds of the city people explain such feeling with mere words?

Thus, life goes on, and people keep hating other people. No one ever questions why they never choose the other way: love.

The streetlamps flicker in the storm. On the deserted road leading to the city's central station, the silent shadow of a wearied soul passes with heavy footsteps. A woman lifts her window blinds and gasps at the sight: why, it is none other than the old, venerable monk. He has returned after many years of pilgrimage. His face is filled with wrinkles, and his skin bears the same shade of coals. The cloth of his faith has faded with time, but his eyes still burn with the bright flame of hope—brighter than ever, thanks to the journeys he's been through and the misery he takes. Suffering child, yes, he has become, and now he's here to witness the downfall of his final test. He is heading toward the Museum of Echoes.

The woman runs out the door with haste. She abandons the shouts of her husband and the cries of her children. The storm is at its peak; there's no guarantee she will be safe out there. The city magistrate won't take responsibility for the disappearance of an ordinary citizen. But she risks it all for the chance to witness a miracle. Her father has told her about the monk in black holy cloth and worn sandals. Her mother has wept over the monk who bowed his head in defeat at the gate of the Museum of Echoes. Now it's her turn to witness the wheel as it rolls forward. Curiosity? No; it is faith.

And many seasoned city people come awake after the woman. They trail behind her in a haze, as if hypnotized—no, rather, as if they have finally been called upon. They follow the monk to the museum's steel gate, queuing after him in a supreme order. The nouveau riche look at the queue from the shelter of their gilded gate, smacking their tongues and shaking their heads at the madness. The crowd of intellects, they think, always leads to destruction. Those whose eyes can see too well risk losing their heads, and the blind will always be leading the blind.

"Oh, venerable monk, sir." The woman is the first to speak. Her voice almost loses its sound in the rain. "Why hast thou come here again to us ignoring fools? Art thou here to lead us to salvation, to rid us of the echoes?"

The monk persists in silence. His eyes keep staring at the gate; the flame within is almost strong enough to melt the steel and burn down the gaudy building with the moss-covered sign, Museum of Echoes. He doesn't speak, but all is understood.

"Oh, venerable monk, sir." A man raises his voice, begging on his knees as many of his contemporaries follow suit. "Please lend us thy strength of will and thy power of wisdom. Please lead us out of this nightmare of ignorance disguised as peace. We beg for thy mercy, oh, venerable monk. Thou art the messiah of the Lord our Creator."

The crowd weeps underneath the monk's feet, but he is immovable. Suffering children, yes, they have become, but their final tests have yet to come, and the monk is not one to pass on their judgment. He knows his place.

"Oh, venerable monk, sir." An elderly woman weeps, her hands holding tightly to the hem of the monk's robe. "Please bestow on us Thy wisdom. A word, nay, a teaching of old. Please deliver us from pain and sorrow. We have been buried so long in willful ignorance."

"Silence." The monk utters his first word. The crowd immediately lowers their heads, praying, waiting for his preaching. "Look ahead and watch. Observe the fall. Innocence is blessed. Ignorance is bliss. Why art thou searching for the things thou possesseth?"

The crowd is stunned under the gentle breeze of the monk's voice. A howl rises, piercing through the night. It is the elderly woman; she is growing hysterical, overcome by a strange burst of emotion. The crowd looks at her, wondering what she has been bearing all these years. The way she has been silently repressing the agony, grudgingly biting back the rebellious words and protests, swallowing her voice, she turns mute, only for her despair to howl so loud, so devastatingly human now. The first woman weeps. She understands the elderly woman's misery. Not so much the feelings, not quite a sympathy— it is simply the same burden borne on the shoulders of any ordinary woman, the burden no writer cares to portray. The man growls, tearing at his hair, asking everyone and no one at all, "What am I possessing?" The question drops amidst the pouring rain, drenches the ordinary ignorance in fuel, ignites the spark of self-doubt, and the crowd goes mad. Some prostrate themselves at the feet of the monk. Others pray on their knees for the forgiveness of their faith and for the pettiness they had in their hearts because life had forced them to be small. The rest cry for salvation, for the second coming of the deity they know will absolve them of sins. Wasn't there a person who said that all sinners would have a future? But wasn't that person condemned severely by a society that was no different than their own?

The monk, witnessing that, only shakes his head in his long-enduring acceptance.

The steel gate stands strong amidst the raging storm. The gleaming surface of the curving Baroque design and the cheap architectural copycat of the imposing Parthenon stare at the maddening crowd in all their stupendous magnificence. The building is thick with the cemented layers of traditional values and the firm foundation of millions of dollars of hierarchy; it is hard to break down a building like that. A normal reader would have invoked Howard Roark's ghost. A wise reader would have watched the thunder strike it down. The wrath of God grows stronger as the wind laughs in the sinister darkness, carrying the sound of fury within its pregnant belly like a prized possession. *Zeus would be proud of His descendants*, the first woman thinks, looking at the pouring rain.

"Oh, venerable monk, sir." The woman turns to the monk in her tired defeat. "What art thou waiting for if not a deliverance?"

"I don't come here to refuse suffering," the monk said, an unperturbed calm showing on his face.

"Then why hast thou come? To laugh at us mortals? Or to justify thy belief?"

"The Lord giveth His children suffering and the Lord forgave them their sins. If the Lord thou art speaking of condones the inflated egos of the few, or the one, then He is no God of mine."

"Oh, venerable monk, sir, thou must have been laughing

since the first brick of this grotesque building was laid." The man bows down, his forehead hitting the hard earth, and he refuses to lift his face up. Something is cracking through his words, and the crowd can feel it running through their veins. It is an unreserved shame. The cowardice is coming back to haunt them again.

"Why must I be laughing?" The monk looks at the man, his eyes wide open, but there's no vision in that startling whiteness. The pity is there in his eyes, but it is veiled by the transparent shadow of apathy. "Thou hast chosen to go thy way. Be proud, as I hath chose mine. We are all suffering. What would be the use of laughing at God's lost children as we all hath become? Hast thou not believed in the faith of the riches? How hast it turned out for thee? I have returned to learn of the test."

"What test, oh, venerable monk, sir?" The first woman speaks, trembling on her knees.

"The test of the stronger faith: between humans and God, I would like to see who will dictate the final gospel. I want to hear the echoes speak."

The monk returns to his impenetrable silence. Together with him, the crowd looks ahead and watches the gate of the Museum of Echoes. The final lost soul is still trapped inside. What faith did she choose? And what will be the result of her test?

The writer plunges herself deeper into the labyrinth of madness and creation. She barely recognizes herself in the darkness. Her voice is lost to the sound of the tempest that is reverberating through the museum's stained-glass windows. She climbs down the staircase, thinking she is going up. When she reaches the top, she thinks she is at the bottom. Her sense of direction is thrown into chaos. She is lost in the labyrinth of her mind. And yet, she still believes that she is on her way out. *The breakthrough*, she thinks, *is somewhere around the corner.* In the first page of a book. Between the covers of some archaic classics. Underneath the lines of a forgotten text. The first edition of an unpublished manuscript. In her passionate insanity, she throws down book after book, forgetting one simple rule. Cormac McCarthy. *The Passenger.* "No matter how much you love the dead, the dead can't love you back."

It is not an obsession. It is not greed. It is a higher indifference she holds toward all things sacred and all things that could be; she wants her name to be remembered. The prizes, the publications, the success records—they are all in the past. She is well aware that in a few years, people will forget her, the same as they will forget any author, writer, penholder. Of course, who would ever remember a story about a vagabond traveling in the dark? She clutches her unfinished story closer to her heart. What she deems as her most valuable possession is nothing but mere waste paper, ready to be thrown into an editor's trash bin any time he sees fit. Holding onto the gilded balcony of the museum, she gazes at the deep spiraling nothingness at the center of the intersecting hallways. *Don't,* she mutters to herself in the crazy haze of a dreamless sleep, not knowing where her life ends and where the nightmare begins, *Don't stare at the abyss.*

The echoes ring in the dark. She fancies she hears them murmur, the secret discussion of the undead, or rather, the ones who long to be dead, to be forgotten, to lay down their lives and rest but who keep being resurrected for generations as the indestructible symbols of what it means to be human. She imagines what they are talking about when they look at her. The sight of a struggling writer flounders in the darkness of her own choosing, not wanting to get out, wishing for a way out, and finally settling for a limbo state because either way, she will end up destroying herself.

Simone de Beauvoir. *The Woman Destroyed.* "It is dreadful to think that behind me my own past is no longer anything but shifting darkness."

The thunder strikes once. The ceiling glass shatters. Pieces of colored crystal fall through the unfathomable, eerie disquietude of the museum. The Victorian chandelier shakes twice, then with a loud creak, it descends into the abyss, bringing with its fall the last light. Darkness holds reign. The writer watches on in absolute despair. Her writing is scattered to the wind. She looks behind her, trying to find Ariadne's thread. Her hands quickly roll up the line; she runs toward the coil, or where she believes the coil still exists. Unbeknownst to her, she is only running in circles, getting lost further in the labyrinth of the many shelves and hallways of the dark museum. She keeps on running, thinking she is getting out, knowing she is being swallowed by the jaws of what other people call the age-old, sweet trap of delusional grandeur.

Gabriel Garcia Márquez. *Love in the Time of Cholera.* "There was no innocence more dangerous than the innocence of age."

Greatness. Legacy. Leaving a mark and striving to be something other than a speck of dust in the barren desert of humanity. Is she wrong to think this? Is she wrong to dream? Her ink has become invisible. Her pages run thin. The words no longer come out of her pen. She lets out a haunting cry as she realizes Ariadne's thread has been cut, and with a missing footstep on a broken staircase, she falls down into the abyss. The end was dictated before the story began.

Outside, the crowd and the monk stand still, watching the

thunderstorm unleash its power. The lightning tears open the sky. The curtains of night part way, allowing the roar of the gods to come through and reach the mortals' ears. Even the nouveau riche are forced to open their blinds and witness the happening. The seasoned city people kneel, their hands clasped tight, eyes closed, praying with soft voices. The chanting of God's name slowly rises to a wave, strong enough to crash through the anchored steel gate. Suddenly, the Museum of Echoes' glass ceiling breaks open. The pages of the writer's notebook pour out like a whirlwind of the last human's attempt at awakening the absurd. A page falls at the monk's feet. He picks it up and reads it out loud to the waiting crowd:

The vagabond looks at his reflection in the mirrors. Though he could not see, there are many people here who can tell him what he looks like now after the long pilgrimage to find himself. One of the voices next to him says he looks like the tallest man on earth, and he beams with pride. Another voice sneers, saying that he looks nothing like a man and more like a monster. He slumps away with sadness, but not for long. Quickly, he finds yet another human, asking for their opinion. The voice tells him he is the smallest man on earth, to which he asks, "Who, then, sir, is the tallest man on earth?"

"Why have you come to ask this of me?"

"Because I want to challenge him. I am becoming. I will be the tallest man on earth after him."

"But you can't."

"Why, oh, sir, pray tell? Don't you have faith?" The vagabond asks, dejected by the voice's defeatism.

"It is because I have faith that I know you can't. There is no tallest man on earth, and no one will become him."

"What about me?"

"Look in the mirror."

"I can't see."

"Look in the mirror."

At that mystical reply, the vagabond looks ahead. He gasps, and with a sharp yelp, he falls dead on the ground. Look in the mirror, he did, and what looked back at him was not the tallest man on earth, nor the smallest man, but a raggedy vagabond. He had spent his whole life searching, only to die on such a simple truth.

A vagabond will always be a vagabond. Much like him, the Lord has spent His suffering teaching humans that bitter pill called faith.

The monk closes his eyes; a single tear trails down his frail left cheek. The crowd waits for him to speak, ready to swallow his words with a fervent hunger. He brushes the page straight, then with careful motions, he places it into the revered open palms of the first woman.

"Oh, venerable monk, sir, what is this for?" she asks. Her hands are shaking, her voice tremulous with fear.

"Take this page as my offering. Thy journey will be long and arduous, child, and suffer thou will. But thy Lord hath come and thy Lord hast spoken. Be a vagabond. Always be a vagabond."

Spoken thus, the monk walks away with decisive steps without looking back. Behind him, the crowd rises, roaring with anger and fury. They crash down the steel gate with sheer willpower, and with the strength of their faith alone, in just one night, they break down the legacy of thousands of years. By the first light of dawn, the Museum of Echoes returns to its rightful state: a pile of bricks and cement layers, with broken staircases and gaudy, gilded balconies. Underneath the wreckage, the corpse of the writer lies on top of the bones of many others like her. Her eyes are tranquil. Her face becomes calm.

After all, she has achieved the end she desires: the greatness of all things is the greatness unto death.

"Every saint has a past, and every sinner has a future."

–– Oscar Wilde

About the Author

Thanh Dinh is a Vietnamese-Canadian writer and poet whose work explores grief, queerness, diaspora, and the sacred violence of survival. Her prose and poetry are known for their lyrical intensity, emotional precision, and fearless intimacy. She is the author of *The Smallest God Who Ever Lived*, *Salt & Ashes*, and *Chronicle of a Love Foretold*, as well as the forthcoming *Love, Anyways: Because the Apple Trees Blossom*. Her work has appeared in literary journals and been recognized for its bold engagement with memory, myth, and the moral weight of love.

You can connect with me on:

🌐 https://writerlybookspub.com
f https://www.facebook.com/writerly.books

Also by Thanh Dinh

The Smallest God Who Ever Lived

A poet kneels before her own ruin and calls it faith.

In this acclaimed debut collection, Thanh Dinh writes through grief, diaspora, and divine disobedience with unflinching grace. *The Smallest God Who Ever Lived* is a gospel for the brokenhearted—a haunting testament to survival, tenderness, and the unbearable beauty of being human. Praised for its emotional ferocity and lyrical precision, this book asks: what remains sacred when love itself becomes a wound?

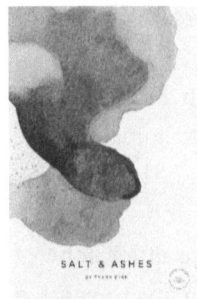

Salt & Ashes: Poems from the Abyss

Every elegy is a love song gone wrong.

Structured like a symphony—Andante, Romanze, Scherzo, and Finale—*Salt & Ashes* dives deep into the fractures of memory, queerness, and grief. Each movement burns with poetic clarity, confronting the ghosts of violence and longing with brutal tenderness. These are not quiet poems; they are the prayers of someone who has already lost everything, yet still sings.

Chronicle of a Love Foretold: A Novel

Two boys, one love the world refuses to forgive.

In the city lights where survival means silence, Dong—a quiet teenager bearing generational trauma—and Simon—a restless dreamer trying to break free from the prison of his perfect life—find refuge in each other's arms. But when their secret is exposed, love becomes both their salvation and undoing. *Chronicle of a Love Foretold* traces the fragile bond between two exiled souls navigating shame, poverty, and the ghosts of the past. Lyrical, unflinching, and devastatingly intimate, Thanh Dinh's debut novel is a portrait of forbidden love and the brutal grace of being seen.

Love, Anyways: Because the Apple Trees Blossom

Even in a ruined world, something still dares to bloom.

In *Love, Anyways*, Thanh Dinh gathers stories of tenderness and defiance—where loneliness becomes a form of beauty, and love persists not because it is easy, but because it must. From forgotten cities to the quiet ache of memory, these stories wrestle with what it means to remain human amid violence, guilt, and grace. A poetic, devastating testament to the endurance of the heart.

Kill My Darling

Some love stories end in forgiveness. This one ends in blood.

When Angela falls for Bambi—a rapper with a haunted past—their passion becomes an apocalypse. *Kill My Darling* is a fever dream of obsession, addiction, and revenge, where the line between devotion and destruction blurs into madness. Told in Dinh's signature lyrical prose, this novel is both a psychological thriller and a requiem for the lost—a story of what love can resurrect, and what it must destroy.